NOT QUITE THE END OF
THE WORLD JUST YET

Also By Peter M. Ball

SHORT STORY COLLECTIONS

The Birdcage Heart & Other Strange Tales

Not Quite The End Of the World Just Yet: Short Stories & Strange
Futures

These Strange & Magic Things: Short Stories

KEITH MURPHY URBAN FANTASY THRILLERS

Exile

Frost

Crusade

MIRIAM ASTER NOVELLAS

Horn

Bleed

ESSAYS

You Don't Want To Be Published & Other Things Nobody Tells
You When You First Start Writing

NOT QUITE THE END OF THE WORLD JUST YET

Short Stories & Strange Futures

PETER M. BALL

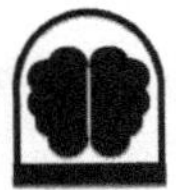

Brain Jar Press
PO Box 6687
Upper Mt Gravatt, QLD, 4122
Australia
www.BrainJarPress.com

This edition Copyright © 2021 by Peter M. Ball; This book was first published by Brain Jar Press, © 2018 by Peter M. Ball. An extension of this copyright page can be found on page 198-199.

The moral right of Peter M. Ball to be identified as the author of this work has been asserted.

All rights reserved. No part of this book may be reproduced in any form or by any electronic or mechanical means, including information storage and retrieval systems, without written permission from the author, except for the use of brief quotations in a book review.

Cover design by Brain Jar Press
Cover Image: Couple Holding Gun Looking At A Giant Robot, Tithi Luadthong/Shutterstock

ISBN: 978-0-6481761-2-1 (Ebook) | 978-1-922479-18-1 (Paperback)

Contents

One Saturday Night, With Angel

If you ask Mike, the problem with the angels is that they smell like laundry powder. They have that real caustic, back-of-the-throat kind of scent that burns itself in. Mike is sick breathing it in twenty-four-seven, and he wants it gone. He's not particularly worried about any of the other stuff.

There's an angel on the roof of the Nite Owl when Mike comes in for the late shift. He thinks it's the same angel that's been following him for six days, but all the angels look the same. The angel is nude, covering its gaunt body with black wings and gauze bandages around the hands and feet. Mike's stuck in the puke-yellow Nite Owl uniform that makes everyone look sick.

Conventional wisdom says six days of seeing the same angel increases your chances of a purging. Mike tries not to worry about it. He's got a graveyard shift, ten 'til morning, the one he traded with Skull last week before the angel showed up. Skull says he's playing a gig with his death-metal band tonight and that's why he can't work. Mike doesn't buy that for a second. No-one plays death-metal after midnight on a Saturday anymore, not unless they've got a death wish.

Not that Mike cares; he likes the nightshift. He waves to the angel.

"Hey," Mike says. The angel crouches down, mute shadow against the sky, wings spread out so they eliminate a broad swathe of stars. People say you're supposed to avoid talking to angels but Mike figures it isn't going to hurt. It's been six days, after all, it's not like anything he does in the next couple of hours will make a difference.

They use fluorescent lights in the Nite Owl. Mike's eyes are raw after a week of being followed by an angel and its smell, so the fluorescents make his eyes water. The entire building creaks every time the angel on the roof moves. Mike takes Patty's spot behind the counter and changes the radio station on the stereo.

"You look tired," Patty says. She's too young for this job, and prone to stating the obvious.

"I am tired," Mike says. "Have a good night, yeah?"

The angel makes people nervous, so the first hour is dead in the water. Nothing happens until Elvis shows up at midnight. Not the real Elvis, he's still dead, just an Elvis whose parents happened to be big fans of the King. Elvis disappears into the fridges at the back of the store, stocking up on the staples that will take him through 'til morning. His next stop is the magazine aisle. Elvis paws through the racks and picks up a *Playboy*. He considers it for a few seconds and looks up at the ceiling, then shakes his head and puts it back. The other side of the aisle is filled with foil-wrapped chocolates. Elvis grabs a fistful of Violet Crumbles and dumps them on the counter.

"Hey," Elvis says.

"Hey," Mike says. He yawns and rubs his eyes. Elvis

shuffles from foot to foot. The sliding doors open up and a small group of club-girls wanders through, fresh off the bus and hungry for hotdogs. Four girls in the group, and one of them is hot, all bare midriff and long legs.

"You got an angel on the roof," Elvis says. He's twenty-six maybe and soft, belly bulging beneath his size-too-large Sex Pistols T. Elvis doesn't want his parents to think he shares their music tastes, and he wants to hide his gut. He has the kind of belly you want to poke.

Mike starts ringing up the Cokes and the chocolate. The angel on the roof shifts its weight again, just a little, and the entire building creaks. One of the girls squeals, the club-girls always squeal, and the floor is full of dropped onions and hotdog buns. The other girls giggle. Mike finishes ringing up the last Crumble bar.

"That's twelve-seventy," he tells Elvis. They look at the mess on the floor by the hotdog bar. Mike says, "Yeah, I might have noticed the angel."

Elvis fishes in his pockets. Then he stops.

"I wanted a pack of cigarettes," he says. "Sorry. Winnie Blues."

Mike turns around and picks up a pack. One of the girls has put a hotdog in the microwave. The smell of melting cheddar starts fighting back against the angel smell. Mike rings up the cigarettes and tosses them into a plastic bag with the Coke. Elvis has noticed the club-girls now. He's gawking at the hot one.

"How long do you reckon it will hang around" Elvis says. "The angel, I mean."

Mike shakes his head.

"They're usually here for a couple of hours, at least," he says. "This one's mine though; it's been following me for days."

"Man, that sucks," Elvis says. "Why the hell did you come to work?"

Mike yawns. "What else are you going to do? Repent? You know how the winged bastards work."

Elvis grins like he does, but he doesn't. All he's got are theories, just like Mike. Just like everyone else. It's stupid, if you ask Mike; all those purges and no-one knows a damn thing for sure. All they've got are theories.

The angel smell is getting worse. The first of the club-girls makes it to the counter. She's carrying two hotdogs, a litre-bottle of Coke, and a purse held open so she can dig for her wallet. It's the hot one. Elvis swallows, really loud and noticeable. Mike rolls his eyes.

"Hey," the girl says. She's a looker, but her voice is a little nasal. Mike doesn't mind that too much when they've got good legs. He probably shouldn't be thinking that on a day like today, but he does.

"Hey," Mike says. Elvis stands there, running fingers through his lank hair. The girl flicks him a quick look and a nervous smile.

"Hey," Elvis says. "Did you see the angel on the roof? He's a beauty, yeah?"

"Sure," the girl says. "I guess. I didn't pay much attention."

She pulls a pack of LifeSavers from the stand by the counter and adds them to her pile.

"I don't really believe in angels," she says.

Mike rings up the LifeSavers and her hotdog. Elvis blinks a couple of times. The girl starts dredging the bottom of her purse for spare change. It's a silver purse, metallic and shiny. It hurts Mike's eyes.

"You're kidding, right?" Elvis says. "About not believing in angels? I mean, they're right there."

"No," the girl says. "There's something there, but I don't have to believe it's an angel."

Elvis looks at Mike. Mike focuses on the cash register. It beeps obligingly as he scans the bottle of Coke.

"So, what, are you stupid?" Elvis says. "What about the purging?"

The girl shrugs.

"Haven't got me yet," she says. She pushes a fistful of change across the counter and picks up her hotdog. She gives Mike a wink. Mike doesn't want any trouble with a crazy woman, not even a hot one.

"Why?" Mike says.

"Why what?"

"Why don't you believe in angels?" Mike says.

The hot girl flashes Mike a smile, just a quick one. She loops the purse on her forearm and picks up the Coke.

"Never do something people advertise on bumper stickers," she says. Elvis shakes his head. The girl waves to her friends in the aisles and points outside.

"Have a nice night," Mike says, and the girl walks outside and flops onto the bench beside the bus stop. She's just inside the light that spills out from the sliding doors of the Nite Owl. She puts her Coke on the concrete and starts eating the hotdog. Elvis stares at her through the glass door.

"Wow," he says.

"Yeah," Mike says.

"She was hot," Elvis says.

"Yeah," Mike says. The other club-girls finish up at the microwave. Elvis has the good sense to shut the hell up while they pay for their food. When they go outside they cluster around the bus stop. There is eating and laughing. Someone points at the angel. They're all wearing big, chunky, dangly earrings.

"What do you reckon her name is?" Elvis says.

"Candace," Mike says. "She seems like the type."

"You think?" Elvis says. "I dunno. I was thinking something a little more traditional. Mary-Anne? Annabelle? Something Anne-ish."

"What about Anne?" Mike says.

"No," Elvis says. He fishes one of the Coke cans out of his bag and opens it. The fizz sparks the air for a few seconds. "She's Anne-ish, but she's not an Anne."

Mike watches the girl through the window. She's a red-head, but he doubts the colour is natural.

"No, I guess not," he says.

The angel on the roof shifts its weight again, and this time it flaps its wings. Mike and Elvis hold their breath, listening to the soft whap-whap-whap of the black feathers. It's too slow for the angel to be taking off, so they start breathing again. Outside, the girls are caught in the thick breeze of the angel's wings. The girl who is probably-not-an-Anne is smoothing her bottle green skirt. The other girls struggle to fix their mussed hair.

"I reckon she's probably a philosophy student," Elvis says, "one of those brainy, existential types in disguise. That's why she doesn't believe in angels."

"Philosophy's dead, remember?" Mike says. He tries not to sound bitter, but it doesn't work. He wishes someone would dim the fucking florescent lights. He wishes the angels smelt like something nicer, like fresh bread or lavender.

"Not altogether dead," Elvis says. "I saw this thing on *Today Tonight* about these rogue classes that still exist, reading Nietzsche and Sartre in secret. Probably a little Camus on the side."

"You think?" Mike says. He's never liked Nietzsche readers, even before the angels. He starts tapping his fingers on the counter, drumming out the chorus to some Adam Ant song on the radio. He checks his watch. Seven hours to go. He can take a break at three. The caustic angel-smell gets stronger, thick and heavy like the angel has started sweating. Mike blinks back tears as the smell works its way towards the back of his throat. He contemplates getting a bottle of water out of the fridge.

"I reckon she's probably a hairdresser," Mike says. "She's got the look."

"You think?" Elvis says. He swills the last few drops of Coke out of the can.

"It's the hair," Mike says. "She's got one of those flick-things going at the end. No-one has those at this time of night, not unless they know what they're doing during the set up."

Elvis rubs his chin and watches the girl who's probably-not-an-Anne.

"I dunno," he says. "She might just have some really good product. They sell product that good."

Elvis pats his pockets, looking for a lighter. One of the girls outside makes a joke, and not-Anne laughs. Her laughter is high and tinkly, like tapping a wine glass.

"I dunno," Elvis says. "A hairdresser. You really reckon?"

"I reckon," Mike says. He yawns without bothering to cover his mouth. The girls have lost interest in their hotdogs by now, but that's okay. No-one can really eat an entire Nite Owl hotdog. Not even when they're drunk. It's a sign of sanity.

"So do you reckon the angel-thing would have worked?" Elvis says. "As a pickup, I mean. If she'd believed in angels."

"No," Mike says.

"No?"

"There's nowhere to go," Mike says. "What do you say after that? Hope we're safe here? Ever seen them purge? When was the last time you went for an absolution?"

"We could talk about the Arrival," Elvis says. "What we were doing, where we were; all that kind of stuff?"

"Downer," Mike says. "Remember the first purge? You really want to start comparing notes, working out who lost who?"

"We could talk about what constitutes a sin," Elvis says. "I mean, that's supposed to be flirty, right? If you can get them talking about something naughty? Anything that gets them thinking in the right direction?"

Mike shakes his head. It's too late to be putting up with Elvis.

"I don't think it works that way," Mike says. "And she wouldn't have gone you regardless. She's hot."

"And I'm not?"

Mike rolls his eyes and Elvis grins. An angel would have purged Elvis years ago if the world was a fair place.

"It used to be easier," Elvis says. "Fuck it. It used to be so much easier."

"Yeah," Mike says. "I guess it did."

The laundry powder angel-smell rolls through the Nite Owl, so strong that both of them have tears in their eyes. They both gag and cough, trying not to breathe. The angel starts to move again. This time the wings are thumping hard and fast, the angel is taking to the air. The entire store creaks. Mike puts both hands on the counter, holding himself steady.

"Shit," Elvis says. "Look at that."

He points a finger through the glass door, towards the bus stop and the club-girls and the angel shadow that falls over them as wings block out the streetlights. The bandaged feet drop down through the frame of the glass doors, cracking the concrete as the angel settles onto the ground. It spreads its black feather wings. It points at the girl who is probably-not-an-Anne. Mike checks his watch, twelve thirty-two. Technically right, but somehow it seems like cheating. Sundays don't really start until you wake up and the church bells are ringing.

"Shit," Elvis says. "She was hot."

The club-girls are screaming. One of them is begging, but not not-Anne. She's just whimpering quietly, tears on her cheeks. The angel hugs her close and the wings start flapping. Lazy flaps, just enough to slowly get back to the roof. There are still a couple of hours 'til dawn, and that means the angel's got to wait. The building creaks again, and a little dust falls from the ceiling.

"Told you," Elvis says. "Philosophy student."

He pops the top of his second can of Coke and unwraps a Violet Crumble. Mike closes his eyes and pretends he can't hear not-Anne whimpering on the roof. He pretends that flutter in his stomach isn't relief. Not-Anne's friends are buzzing outside, all bleating cries and desperate mobile calls. Like the cops give a damn when divine retribution is involved.

The angel will be carrying not-Anne into the sunrise and no-one will do a goddamn thing. That's how purging works. The angel carries you away, and no-one knows what happens after that, but Mike's willing to bet it's not good. The angels look sad when they're carrying people away, and that's never a good sign.

Six hours and forty-two minutes until Mike can go home. Another three hours and twelve minutes until he gets his break. The angel is back on the roof with a hot girl held in his arms, waiting for the sunrise so he can take off and no-one will see not-Anne again. Elvis finishes his Violet Crumble and pulls the plastic rapper off his pack of Blues.

"Outside," Mike says.

"Come on," Elvis says. He has a cigarette between his lips and a lighter in his hand.

"Seriously," Mike says. "Out."

He jerks his thumb towards the sliding door and the hysterical girls. He wishes he could go out and smoke with Elvis. The angel smell in the Nite Owl is so thick Mike wants to spit it out, again and again and again.

To Dream Of Stars: An Astronomer's Lament

The first time he sees the Royal Observatory he is three days shy of his twelfth birthday. It's spring, a clear night, the stars unveiling themselves in small groups as the sky overhead grows dark.

The tower rises from the hills, dominating the uneven horizon, a crooked silhouette against the twilight. The glowing dome at the tip points at the emerging stars, the length of the tower twisted like the four-joined finger of a great and alien hand. He feels the strangeness of the building, a discordant note casting echoes in the chambers of his heart, but the otherness calls to him regardless. John Flamsteed is promised to God in both body and spirit, but he knows his heart and mind now belong to that tower forever.

"Eyes off it," his father orders, cuffing the boy across the back of the head, and John falls forward, clinging to the horse's mane to keep himself in the saddle. The older Flamsteed rides on, glaring at the observatory. "It's evil," his father says, "and dangerous yet. You will not look at it. You will not even think of it, or the creatures that dwell within. Do you understand?"

John Flamsteed nods, used to obedience without understanding. His father sees evil where other men see nothing, though perhaps this once John can see the hint of corruption his father fears. He averts his gaze, but the tower remains. It looms on the fringe of his vision, a constant threat. The sight of it pulls at his heart, luring him as though he's been hooked on a silvery strand of twine wrapped around the tower's domed tip.

They have three days of business in town, just long enough for John to hear the stories. He absorbs them, one by one, the details coalescing as he weaves rumor and folk-tale together. There are those that tell him the yellow texture of the tower comes from tiles made of dragon bone, that its twisting mass is held upright by prayer and dark magic. The accusations of magic perturb him, an affront to both God and reason, but he listens and nods and asks again when the moment presents itself. There are folk-tales aplenty to hear, but none to satisfy his thirst for comprehension.

On their final night in town, his birthday, John Flamsteed skulks out of the room he shares with his father. The moon is a thumbnail sliver overhead, a sliver so brief its presence barely registers against the scattered wash of stars. John Flamsteed stumbles through the unfamiliar streets, toes catching the rough cut cobblestones, tripping his way into the open fields and the hills beyond. The air smells fresh and clean, but the aftertaste is sour. He climbs the unfamiliar slopes, his young body straining against the rough terrain hidden by darkness.

The Observatory serves as a compass, allowing him to orient himself against the empty darkness the tower casts against the endless stars. Eventually John stands at the base, staring up at a tower tall enough to brush against sky. John Flamsteed examines the pale shingles, stands close enough that he can reach out and touch their worn exterior with the tips of his young fingers. They feel like the smoothed edge of a predator's incisor, noble, deadly and beautiful in a single moment.

He thinks of the stories the townsfolk tell about children raised to the Astronomers Royal, kidnapped and replaced by changelings, stripped of their humanity by the Astronomer's training. In the lonely light of the thumbnail moon, John Flamsteed makes a promise. He will return here, one day, free from the shackles of his father's assumptions. He will give himself over to the stars and the Others, all in the name of God and his country. Damn the impossibilities, he will enter the tower and join the ranks of the Astronomers Royal.

All he can see is the long teeth, clusters of bone-yellow fangs that shine as they jut away from her gums. His eyes are closed but the image stays with him, echoing through his head as he waits for the first teasing bite. He can feel the length of her tongue, the cat-lick rasp of it as she works her way along his thigh. The image of those teeth growing larger and stronger as the tongue works up his leg, the damp warmth of her breath sliding over him. He wonders what it will feel like, that first piercing bite. What will happen when she starts ripping and rending his flesh while he's trapped beneath her bulk.

The Other begins her work. There is no hint of teeth in their interaction. No teasing bites or sharp incisors against his skin, but the quiet menace of their arrangement lingers. It is difficult to forget those teeth, even for one such as him, trained and equipped to handle the intricacies of the exchange.

She raps his forehead with a six-knuckled hand, uses the brief flash of pain to focus his attention. He forces his eyes open and meets her gaze, staring into her gold-flecked pupils that have seen more than he can imagine. He ignores the quiet menace of her grin. This is, after all, what he longed for as a boy. It would not do to fail the public trust after all he has done to earn it.

"Focus," she hisses. Her voice is awkward to listen to, a croak full of slant inflections and awkward syntax. "You are not here. Your thoughts on the moment must be here. Very important. Focus."

She lowers her head and the tongue works its way across the plump line of his stomach, leaving a trail of sticky fluid in its wake. He forces himself to focus, to keep his eyes on her. He lets the image of her teeth dissolve.

"It's important," she says, murmuring, the tongue working at the fold of his belly button. "Must be present. Must be here. To lose focus would be bad, very bad. Very bad for both of us."

And Flamsteed swallows, just once, acutely aware of the way his Adam's apple bobs and dances with the gesture. He focuses on the moment, on the rasp of the tongue and the needle pricking as she suckles, the pain that starts boiling through his chest. He focuses on the long teeth and the tongue built for sucking marrow, the tongue that coils around him like a serpent as the Other explores his body. He keeps his focus and he watches her, gives himself over to the moment.

"Good," the Other says. "Good. All is well. Now stay with me. Stay with me. Stay with me through the pain."

He learns the danger of ambition early. There is a stray moment as they rode home; his father asks about the future and Flamsteed answers honestly.

"I wish to become an astronomer," he says, and the statement is followed by the stinging pain of a backhanded blow, the whistle of the wind as he tumbles into the dirt.

"Foolishness," his father says. "It is an insult that you consider such a thing."

And perhaps it is. John Flamsteed curses his own

inattention, the foolishness of revealing himself so soon. It's easier than acknowledging the foolhardy desire, that he wishes for something that cannot be earned, that can only be bequeathed by the Other taking a child at birth. His lip drips blood as he climbs back into the saddle, dark spots staining the cracked leather. His father's dark eyes are on him, blazing with the angry flame of the Almighty, and John subsumes the pain with practiced ease. He will not seethe in front of his father, will not allow himself to be distracted by thoughts of the tower.

He looks forward with due attention, keen eyes tracing the winding road leading him to a future filled with grain and trade and the secrets of malt. His father lectures him through the endless hours it takes to reach home: on the evils of the tower, on the devilry of the outsiders who journey there, on the taint that lingers over those who live in its shadow. As always, the lecture revolves around the same words: "Better we had destroyed the place when his Majesty fell in the war. Better that the heavens had remained the palace of God alone."

And through it all John Flamsteed nods, dabbing his bloody lip until the dried crust forms. He probes the small wound with his tongue, feels the tiny spark of pain that exists beneath the chrysalis of hardened blood. He can endure this, if it is necessary. John Flamsteed defines himself by his ability to endure, to survive the rigors of life as his father's successor.

And that night, as he slumbers, he dreams of the tower. The Royal Observatory, the stars above it, the quiet thrum of its walls when he placed a palm on its surface. He wakes an hour before dawn, sweating and heavy under the covers of his bed. One hand is raised to press the wound on his lip, to let the pain burn beneath the fleshy pad of his fingertip.

• • •

The sharp nails pierce his flesh, digging in below the surface, drawing out a feeling that's almost pain, right on the edge of it, a sharp bite that reminds him of stabbing his finger with the nib of his finest pen. John Flamsteed remains still, his breathing shallow, trying not to disturb his lover's concentration. He feels the fluid seeping into the membranes of his skin, spreading out like an ink-splotch on wet paper.

Something in the back of his mind, some scrap of his brain that struggles to retain a semblance of the ordinary, tells him that he should be panicking. It's a voice he's learned to ignore many lovers ago, a voice that's subsumed in the name of duty. Flamsteed lies back, soaks into the hard mattress. He sighs, unsure if it's prompted by pain or contentment.

"Turn," she orders. This one's voice vibrates like a mosquito's wing, high-pitched and delicate. He rolls over and feels sharp fingernails walking the length of his back, each step another needle-prick. There is a faint stirring of real pain now, down beneath the layers of muscle; a dull ache in the hollows of his bones, the first real register of his body protesting the intrusion.

"Still," she says, caressing the nape of his neck. One finger lingers on the hollow, the point where cranium and spine connect, the same place a hunter strikes when he wants to kill a rabbit. Flamsteed knows better than to tense, knows the pain it will earn him if he attempts to resist penetration. His body stiffens anyway, an ancient reflex he thought conquered years ago. He wonders if it's a sign of age, this inability to control his base reactions. It is only a matter of time before his role is assumed by a younger man, before his wrinkled flesh will refuse to obey him or absorb the rigors required by his duties.

"Now," she says. His neck is stiff when she penetrates, the crisp point of her nail cutting through the taut sinew. The pain that washes through him is magnificent, a sweeping agony that leaves him with the coppery taste of blood in his mouth. Something drips from his nose, making it hard to breathe. He

grits his teeth and draws breath through them, waiting the pain out. The nail is removed, a swift withdrawal accompanied by the wet suck of flesh drawing closed.

A moment later he is numb, the pain driven out by a sweep of frostbite that leaves him shuddering. The universe resolves around him, points of pale light superimposed over the walls of the room, silver-white spots that gradually congeal into familiar constellations.

For a few brief moments, he can feel the universe spreading through his capillaries. He runs his fingers across his ebony skin, tracing the pull of the stars as they rotate around him. He understands, for the first time, the way they pull against the universe, each star determined to draw everything in and shine, alone, as a perfect centre. Once he orients himself, it's possible to make out familiar constellations and old discoveries, the faint glow of 12 Monocerotis and 24 Tauri, the powder-bright dot of 3 Cassiopeia more distinct than he's ever seen her.

He wishes for a sheaf of paper, some means of annotating the exact locations while he has them in such close proximity. By the time he inks a quill they are gone, fading away until his wrinkled flesh is as pale as the moon against the midnight sheets.

"Done," she says. She brushes her nails against one another, sets them tinkling like crystal chimes as she rises. "Your reward, Astronomer, for all you have discovered."

Flamsteed simply nods, weary. He wants to say something, to thank her, but the words do not come.

His father's house runs on strict cycles: six days for business, one day for faith. John forfeit's sleep to his ambition, embracing the freedom to watch the heavens while his father slumbers. He begins his career without details or training, no numbers or names or theories to build on. Life in father's household has no room for stars, no books beyond the accounting ledger and the Bible on the shelf.

Flamsteed builds his first star chart from the night sky visible through the bedroom window, a square frame surrounding three-hundred-and-twenty-nine sparkling dots of light, each memorized and catalogued without the help of paper. Travel with his father becomes a curious pleasure after this, allowing him to study the night through unfamiliar portals, quilting the celestial maps together like the scraps used in a patchwork. His understanding grows as the years pass, each patch constructed from the safety of a new bed, each memory as square and neat as a window frame. He tells no-one what he's doing. The stars he studies for himself alone.

He encounters his first book on astronomy at fourteen, its yellowing pages full of crudely sketched constellations, archaic and constructed without the benefit of the Other's machines. John is fascinated by the childish depictions of the sky, the graceful waltz of the heavens superimposed on straight lines. He closes his eyes and transposes the dots of ink to the sky, tracing their patterns on the canvas of his mind for later study.

He reads for an hour, savouring the experience, the elder Flamsteed discussing business in a nearby parlour, too engrossed in the deal to register John's absence. John commits the pages to memory, as easy as breathing, aligns them with the patchwork he's built over the years.

He acquires his first true book on astronomy three years later, each page pristine and carefully choreographed, the work of the Royal Observatory and the Astronomers whose ranks he still dreams of joining. Flamsteed hides it under his bed, stores it in a small crate still touched with the sour scent of old grain, the book wrapped in waxed paper to protect it from mildew.

It is not long before it's joined by other tomes, by telescopes and star charts he constructs in the night.

They have bypassed the formalities, the flagellation that leaves red welts spiralling across his back like the distorted arms of a newborn galaxy, his limbs crisscrossed with cuts and red lines of inflamed flesh. Flamsteed grits his teeth against the pain, against the soft suckle of her lower appendages. She is pulling herself forward on long and muscular tentacles, each looping grasp giving her new purchase, dragging her bulk through the viscous liquid until she can settle it over Flamsteed's torso.

Tears are permitted in this encounter; discreet trails of saltwater flowing over his craggy cheeks until they merge with the viscid muck of the pool. The salt burns at his raw skin, painfully warm against the cool weight of the sea-green slough covering his body. She moves easily through the thick liquid, reaching out with one of her lower appendages to trace the line of his tears. Flamsteed doesn't flinch from the bone-hooked tip of her tentacle, doesn't shudder as she runs it across his softened flesh.

He rakes the squamous bulk of her body with his fingers, acutely aware of the futility of penetrating her scales with his blunted, human nails. One hand working its way down the double-boned ridge of her spine, the second caressing the open expanse of her torso. She thrums beneath his touch, a dull echo deep beneath the cavernous mass of her chest, extremities writhing in a politely simulated act of pleasure. Flamsteed rakes again but cannot break the thick flesh. She will be disappointed, he knows that. He remembers her from her last visit.

They proceed, politely, playing out the exchange that's expected of them. Flamsteed chides himself for the lack of foresight, for making contact without preparing the required prosthetics, for limiting himself to merely human physical abilities. He has reduced the exchange to simple choreography for the first time in a decade. They will replace him now, dubbing him too old. The thought terrifies him more than he can say.

Flamsteed's nocturnal studies manifest in exhaustion, prompting others to regard him as sickly for the remainder his childhood. His father deems him too weak for college, igniting furious arguments with his son.

Flamsteed clings to his dreams. Letters are written in secret, the necessary books acquired by friends and smuggled into the house. By the time he is permitted to walk into Cambridge Halls, twenty-three and handsome despite his nocturnal pallor, he possessed more knowledge than many who propose to instruct him in the ways of the stars.

He petitions the Queen and the Royal Observatory every year after graduation, his letters echoing the sentiments of a hundred other astronomers who have studied and dreamed as he has. There is a call, a hunger, pervading the Empire, for the secrets of the conquering Others and the Astronomers who serve them.

At thirty, John Flamsteed is the first man to be accepted into the ranks of the Astronomers Royal, his petitions supported by a catalogue of undiscovered stars that's unmatched by any within or without the Royal Observatory. He is first full-grown human to be initiated, the first Astronomer raised outside with an understanding of humanity.

He meets his first Other in the Astronomer's tower, deemed ready after three years of training and preparation. The Other looms over him, her pale face like a narrow sliver of moon, silver stars shining from the empty canals of her eyes.

They taught him the rituals needed to control his

instincts in the face of the unknown, but he feels fear despite the training, the dry taste in his mouth and the chill running through his trembling legs. There is something primal there, a quiet voice screaming for him to flee. It takes courage to stand at the ready, to stare into the endless void of those eyes.

He takes comfort in the void, the gaze that resembles his beloved stars.

Most Astronomers fail in this moment, unable to sublimate their fear. It is death to fail, he knows this, and Flamsteed forces himself to stay, to remain steady as the luminous hand strokes his clenched jaw. The air is thick with humidity, the Other's wildflower scent mixing with the flickering taint of tallow. He forces himself to breath normally, to ignore the lightning-sharp tingle that accompanied the Other's presence. He holds firm as she caresses his face, leans in to study him like a prize horse, forcing his mouth open to check his teeth.

There is no offering in this first encounter, no contact beyond the gentle touch of her fingers, but the solemnity of the moment digs deep into Flamsteed's chest. This, John Flamsteed is sure, lies at the very heart of the evil his father saw in the Observatory; this moment when man may brush against the divine without seeing God behind it.

There is an afterglow with this breed, an ambient luminescence that projects the path of her stellar journey across the domed ceiling. John considers the unfamiliar stars, watching a new sky spread out, magnified by the complex array of curved lenses and glass arrays built into the dome.

There is a beauty to its endless tranquillity, to the stars that twinkle in the boundless regions of space, and in their absence are spaces that even the Others do not visit. Even after all these years, after all the homage and services he's performed, this sight awakens the same quiet awe within him.

The Others tell the Astronomers that the darkness was infinite, stretching on forever in an eternity of empty space. It is only in this room that Flamsteed can comprehend what that may mean. He thinks about the endless, the subtle thrill of pleasure with every new quasar that is found. Thirty years in the observatory and there is still no end to it, no point in the eternal distance that could be the end of a long journey.

And for the first time he wonders if the Others truly do come from stars, all of them connected as the Others claim.

Or whether the gaps in their knowledge speak of some other truth entirely.

John Flamsteed delights in charting unfamiliar stars, studying them and recording them in the neat ledgers that line the walls of his cell. Innumerable ledgers, leather-bound and hand-crafted, their pages filled with neat script and a careful record of what has been found. The legacy of three-dozen years of Astronomy in the name of the Queen, so many years of research and still so much to find.

He is forty-five when he meets the first Astronomer to train as he has trained, another outsider named Edmund Halley whose brilliance has given him access to the tower just as John earned his own place among the Astronomer's Royal. Flamsteed is forty-seven when he first hears the name *Terra Optimus* whispered in the halls, forty-eight before he realizes that the dissidents have sympathizers amongst the ranks of the Astronomers. John Flamsteed struggles to comprehend the logic behind such a group, to comprehend a world without the Others and their gifts of the stars and the Observatory; it seems tantamount to madness.

Yet he contemplates the possibilities late at night,

ignoring the insistent tug of sleep just as he's done since childhood. He fills his journals with sketches in addition to the charts and the stars, recording notes about all the Others he's encountered. Every night he considers the question, *what if,* conceiving of ways to continue his work if he was suddenly bereft of the Observatory and the Others and the gifts they have offered him.

Later still, in the moments before sleep, he offers up silent prayers that his plans are never needed.

He finds Edmund Halley waiting for him in the main Observatory, the younger man paging through Flamsteed's journal. There is something about Halley that Flamsteed finds disagreeable, an unfamiliar cockiness that seems unseemly, even here. The sight of him touching the annotated pages of the journal fills Flamsteed with fear. He fights the itching need to slap the leather covers closed on Halley's fingers.

"Halley," Flamsteed says, the deep croak of his voice causing the younger astronomer to start. Despite his five years of service in the tower, Edmund Halley is not yet ready for anything. It isn't a good sign; the ability to react, to adapt without surprise, is vital to the astronomer.

"John," Halley says nervously, one hand scratching the back of his head. He shuffles across the room, right hand extended, thin lips drawn into a tight, controlled smile. Flamsteed takes the offered hand, shaking it with disdain, his skin crawling as he makes contact. As though Halley were one of the Others, Flamsteed thinks. As if he were just as alien as they.

"I've been reading your journals," Halley says. "Impressive work, I must say. You're to be commended on your diligence."

There is no passion in Flamsteed's cold stare, just a quiet distaste that the conversation has lasted this long. Halley refuses to wither beneath John's gaze when Flamsteed doesn't respond.

"Well, yes," Halley says. "Impressive; a work of genius, if you'd prefer. There has been talk, among the younger astronomers. Some rumbles about distributing your notes."

"For the good of the Empire?" Flamsteed says.

Halley smiles and nods, ignoring the dangerous tone. "Yes, for the good of the Empire. Quite right."

It is a cool day, even behind the insulated stone of the Astronomers' tower. John Flamsteed blinks in the momentary silence.

"No," he says.

"John." Halley looks around, as though preparing to share a secret. "John, this is important. This isn't about us, the astronomers. Your journal represents the most significant catalogue of Other forms known, details beyond the dreaming of any Astronomer half your age. We need this information, urgently."

John Flamsteed's anger is a quiet spark, smouldering with urgency. "No," he says firmly, leaving no room for discussion.

"John," Halley says, but he stops when he hears the hint of a growl in Flamsteed's voice.

He is permitted to meet Her Majesty when he is fifty-three, escorted via carriage to the aging cathedral that has become her throne room. There is a silence beneath the hammer of the horse hooves, an empty space that leaves John Flamsteed alone with his thoughts.

He watches the great building through the window of the carriage. It was God's place, once, but the cathedral now houses the stuff of stars. It is the home of Her Majesty, first among the Other-kin, the great lady who brought the Other to England and awarded the Astronomers her tower. As the carriage thunders into town, the great cathedral looming in the forefront of his vision, John Flamsteed is surprised to find himself weeping.

Her Majesty is a leviathan of pale flesh, her vast bulk expanding to spill over the arms of her throne. She does not speak, but her presence weighs against Flamsteed's mind like the roar of the ocean. *You are the Astronomer Flamsteed.*

"Yes."

You are the first of a new breed, the first willing to sacrifice in exchange for knowledge. It is a great thing, Lord Astronomer, a step forward for your people.

Flamsteed stands in the ancient church and stares.

There were concerns about your appointment, about your ability to survive the rigours required of the post. Was it worth it, Lord Astronomer? The sacrifices you have made?

Flamsteed can feel his stomach boiling, the nausea rising up like steam escaping a kettle. He keeps his mind calm, contemplating Her Majesty's question in secluded pockets of thought, places he has learned to keep hidden from the mental prying of the Other. It occurs to him, for the first time, that he does not wish to know the answer to this.

"It is a difficult question, Majesty. You ask me for conjecture when you have rewarded the Order for their pursuit of proof."

The mound of flesh boils, folds in on itself as Her Majesty rolls forward. Flamsteed watches as a great eye forms amid the flesh, a violet orb shot with a fistful of stars.

We ask for opinion, Lord Astronomer, nothing more. Indulge us, we command you. Give us your answer.

His scars ache, a hundred niggling bites of pain that stretch out across his skin, the cost of too many nights in the open chambers that look up into the stars. There is a hollow feeling that accompanies the pain, an emptiness that spreads through his limbs like the endless dark of the night sky.

"You gave us the stars, Majesty. Is there any price that is not worth that?"

Her Majesty's great eye stares at him, an open window to the universe. Flamsteed stares back and wonders which of the multitude of lights she descended from.

She towers over him, her body composed of insect limbs and chitin skin that gleams in the candlelight, her faceted eyes studying him with detached interest. It is a new breed of Other, the first unfamiliar genus he's seen in years.

John Flamsteed holds his breath as her needle-sharp proboscis penetrates the flesh below his nipple. There is pain, there is almost always pain when dealing with the other, but he expected the heavy appendage to gash flesh like a knife-blade rather than sting like a mosquito bite. He waits with apprehension, breath burning in his lungs, offering a quiet prayer that this time the narrow length will find the space between his ribs. He watches her burrow through the flesh and the layers of muscle, searching for the fleshy sack of his right lung. He cannot breathe until the lung is penetrated, cannot draw breath until she is ready to breathe with him, but penetration takes time and he can already see the star-filled sky of his childhood encroaching on the fringes of his vision, narrowing his perception to a single tunnel that shrinks until there is nothing more than the faceted eyes that keep staring.

The penetration occurs, a popping sensation that leaves him deflated and lethargic. He starts heaving his chest, trying to swallow air, but all he can feel is the quiet pull of her proboscis, the sucking sensation as she breathes in the air of his lungs. He forces himself to concentrate, forces his body to recognize that he isn't choking, but the empty sensation in his chest will not be ignored. He struggles, just a little, enough to give her pleasure. He forces himself to remember the stricture, the litany that all

Astronomers are taught before they are paired with their first Other: we are the servants of the universe, sacrificing ourselves for the gift of the stars; we exist for her pleasure, for our knowledge relies upon their pleasure; we do not ask, do not question, in this moment we belong to her, always to her, and we are their lovers. This is the price we pay to keep our people safe. This is the cost of learning about the darkness.

Flamsteed forces himself to ignore the unspoken advice at the end of the litany, the careful implication that every Other is female. To consider them anything else is unthinkable, even among men who touch the unthinkable day after day.

She reaches the moment of pleasure, quiet moans vibrating along the needle that penetrates him, the black heat of her climax filling the air with the fetid stench of rotting eggs. Flamsteed twists beneath her, pinned on the delicate needle that penetrates him, holding his_tongue while he waits for the moment of release.

Flamsteed is dead fifteen years when the Observatory falls. It is the beginning of the revolt, the end of Her Majesty's rule. The yellow-tiled stone ruptures with the force of a dozen explosions, each carefully placed at important junctures that will bring the great tower low. The long finger of stone bends, twisting as it falls. The stones warp and crumble under their own weight, bearing the crystalline tip of the great tower down until it shatters against the earth. There is a slow inevitability to its fall, like a breath long-held suddenly free to be exhaled. The tremor of its impact roars through Greenwich town, shattering windows and kicking up dust. Flamsteed does not live to see it, but it is his notes that make this possible.

They say it was Halley who fired the first shot, setting taper to the fuse that brought the tower down. They say it was Newton who waged the great war, who brought weapons and worse to the rebels who fought to take Her Majesty down. They say little enough of John Flamsteed, remembering him for less, but the Astronomers Royal continues even after the fall of the Others. We chart courses for the ships we discover and negotiate treaties with those who come after. We prepare Britannia for the other worlds, for the depths of space and beyond. We use Flamsteed's work to determine from where the next attack will come. He studied them and understood, charting their strengths and desires, treating them like the stars he so loved. We say it was Flamsteed that provided the means of Her Majesty's death, for all that it was Halley who put plan into action.

On the anniversary of his death we lie flowers on Flamsteed's tombstone; white lilies resting against a yellow stone taken from the tower he loved.

We mourn him and revere. We promise we shall not forget.

The Last Thing Said Before Silence

I rented the room on the top floor of The Laughing House, so I had a good view as they came to take Mister Kappec away. They floated down the street, two-by-two, held aloft by red balloons tied to thick copper belt-buckles; four-and-twenty barefoot mimes with milk-pale feet, their long toe-nails scraping against the bitumen when they drifted too low. Black-clothed, ghost-haired mimes with empty faces and white gloves, their hands moving in perfect unison even as their discordant formation drifted against the wind. They didn't break ranks until they hit Kappec's yard, until the leader floated up to the front door and knocked three times.

"They're here," I said, and Patrice's breathing went quiet. She lay on my bed, book folded against her chest. I slid a cigarette from the packet on the windowsill and rolled it between my fingers. The mime knocked again, and Mister Kappec opened his door wearing a singlet and black running shorts. His chest hair poked free at the neckline, black and wiry. He wasn't wearing shoes. The lead mime held Kappec's gaze and gestured towards the temple on the hill with both hands, sweeping a path through the gathering crowd. It was an invitation to take the easy way out, to go quietly.

Kappec tried to run for it instead.

They stopped him. The leader of the mimes held up a white-gloved hand, the palm flat, and Kappec slammed into something, rebounding off the empty air with blood streaming from his nose. He retreated into his house, scrambling for the front door and slamming it shut. The mimes watched him go, silent and smiling. "He's not going quietly?" Patrice asked. I shook my head, and she put her book down, padding across the dusty floorboards to peer through the crack in the curtain. "Good for him."

The leader of the mimes blew a long, silent note on a whistle we couldn't see. The air grew still, the mimes bobbing on their balloons. They raised their white-gloved hands and Patrice took notes, scribbling and sketching on a battered pad.

The process of destroying someone with mime could be quick, but the Silent Militia rarely chose that option. They preferred a slow, torturous death; an example to friends and neighbours. Patrice spent two weeks watching Robert Kappec's demise, monitoring every movement the mimes made as they maintained the siege.

On the first day they erected the walls; forty-eight hands reaching out and pressing a barrier into existence, invisible but tangible. They boxed him in, pushing the wall tight around the small shack. Killing via box was indirect, the result of suicide or starvation, but the mimes tortured the condemned for the duration. They sustained themselves through the siege by miming feasts into existence, filling the street with the aroma of a sumptuous banquet that only they could see and taste. They played dirges on invisible violins, sending a wave of grief through the street even though we couldn't hear the mournful tune. Sometimes they mimed fear, hands pulled tight against their chins as they stared in open-mouthed terror at the sky, and we could hear Kappec screaming from inside his prison.

He lasted fourteen days before the screaming stopped and the mimes left. Patrice was standing by the window as they floated away, drifting back towards the dark shadow of the Leviathan that had loomed over the city since the invasion began. "He should have gone with them," I said. "It would have been faster, at least."

"Better to die caged than to follow them to the temple." Patrice turned, sneering at me. "It's slower, but there's dignity in it. The temple is worse; to be sacrificed like that, given to their master—"

She shuddered. "Forget it."

"Maybe it's not as bad as you think."

She glared at me, her eyes cold. "I need to make a report."

Patrice saw herself out, leaving me alone in the silent room. I slept easy for the first time in days.

I think Patrice and I stopped loving one another in the days prior to the invasion. She stayed with me, in the aftermath, because duty demanded it.

In truth, I held no faith in Patrice's revolutionaries. The invasion, when it had come, was sudden and complete. One evening we went to bed and by the morning the Leviathan was there, its vast shadow stretched out across the city and its servants floating through the streets. For a moment, nothing changed. Then there were temples and an oppressive need for silence, the lines of red-ballooned mimes whispering reports into the Leviathan's vast ear. Our subjugation was a ripple that spread through the city, all the panic and resistance processed in seconds and gone once the Silent Militia moved in. The mimes floated down, angry and silent. There was miming, real miming, and they herded people away to be sacrificed at the feet of our conqueror.

There were many Leviathans, shadowy masses that dwarfed the towering buildings of our greatest cities. Each is unique and demented, sending forth their personal armies to keep the peace. In London the great beast is served by cats; in Krakow the streets are patrolled by clockwork golems with silver-bright eyes. In this city, we are watched by the mimes, lean men with silent faces and a precision of gesture. We became muted, a city of whispers and light steps, of frightened glances at the sky before any conversation took place.

I noticed it most at the bar: people stopped talking as they drank; they communicated their hellos with grunts and nods. We had grown to fear sound: the clatter of a dropped spoon was reason enough for censure. Laughter was an offense from which few people recovered.

Patrice still believed in freedom; she laughed because it was an act of rebellion. She scorned me for falling into silence like the rest of the chattel, never questioning my motives. And perhaps there was no fall. Perhaps I embraced the silence willingly, for all it was was a tool of the mimes. I used it as a means to taunt her, transforming her presence in my bedroom into an act of stoic duty.

I knew enough to fear the mimes. I'd been accosted, out on the street, in the early days of the occupation. I was walking and the mimes drifted down, four of them floating around me in a square formation. They were terrifying when seen up close. Their eyes were too large, pupils the size of dark coins that never focused on one thing. The Militia studied me, saying nothing. I clutched a brown-paper parcel in my hand; good bacon, from the days when such a thing was possible. The lead mime crooked his head and leaned in, placed his long nose close to mine. So much of the mime's presence was characterized by absence: I could not smell his breath; I could not feel its warm weight against my cheek. Yet the greasepaint that covered the pock-marked face was thin; I could see streaks of pink flesh against the white. The close proximity of the mimes frightened me. When they touched me the world shivered.

It was after my encounter that I was contacted by others who scorned Patrice's revolution. And yet, I feared. I refused their call for a long time.

She was gone for three weeks, making her report. I worried, listening to the whispers and the rumours, waiting for news of a bombing on the outskirts or a new safe-house where noise was still possible. I watched the mimes floating across the skyline, turned away when they looked in my direction. I wondered and I fretted. Every act of a rebellion is a question for those left behind: could she return? Would she? I contemplated the answers, twisted them inside-out. I drank at work, recklessly, heedless of the danger. Drunks were easy prey for the mimes, prone to loud discourse and song. Three weeks. Patrice didn't send word. When she came home she was accompanied by Nicholas; a tall man, a sad face. He had a mustache that dribbled around the corners of his mouth.

"Laughter is no longer enough," she said. "We move onto the next phase, a truer expression of joy." Nicholas smiled at me. He had crooked teeth. "You should go," Patrice said. "In the name of the revolution."

I declined. I knew better, but I stayed regardless. I said nothing as they kissed; nothing as their moaning echoed through the long halls of the house. When it became too much I retreated to the Café Rue Morte, and waited there until Nicholas found me. Red-faced Nicholas and his crooked teeth, his mournful mustache and the patina of sweat on his brow. "It is done," he said, and his voice whistled in his hollow throat. He looked at me with such sorrow, such hurt about what he'd been invited to do. "It is safe to return. I am sorry, my friend. The cause."

"Yes," I said. I was drinking a flat white that had gone cold while I fumed. "Always for the cause."

Nicholas sat at my table, his back to the eastern outskirts. I watched the shadowed bulk of the Leviathan looming over his left shoulder, the mimes floating around its head, whispering secrets into the malformed ear. Nicholas reached across the table and took my hand. "Reconsider," he said. "It's not too late."

He smiled at me, showing off the teeth. I looked away and said nothing.

There were some who preferred the silence because it gave them time to think, but for many the silence was numbing: one did not have to think, did not have to rant, did not have to feel any fury when faced with the injustice of the occupation. You could listen to the city: the squeak of the trams trundling along their tracks, or the sound of soft shoes pressing against the concrete. The balloons of the mimes creaking as they drifted past, soft rubbery squeaks heralding their presence as they floated through the streets.

When it became too much to bear I chose action over laughter. I had little faith in Patrice and her subversions; the laughter; the moans; the raised voices in public spaces. When I chose to give in, to take my part in the resistance, I placed my faith in those who used more tangible methods.

I acquired a gun, a Beretta automatic bought in the back room of the bar, from an elderly man wearing heavy jackets and carrying an attaché in faded brown leather. He was a friend from the underground, and he wore the weapons strapped to his chest, fastened by white crosses of medicinal tape. The weapon cost less than I'd expected: two bottles of vodka, not even the good stuff; a fistful of worn bills that had lost meaning in the days since the invasion.

"You wanna a silencer?" he asked me. "Good idea, these days. You don't wanna attract attention." I held the heavy weapon up, stiff-armed and posing. I closed my right eye and squinted down the barrel. I closed both eyes and imagined the heavy roar, the echo cutting through the muted city.

"It's good," I said. "I'll take it just as it is."

"It'll be loud. Especially now."

"I want it loud," I told him. I put the gun down on the table and looked at it, admiring the sleek curves. I picked it up again. It was heavy and smelt like oil. The salesmen grunted and opened his attaché, stashing the red-capped vodka bottles among its depths. He watched me shift my stance, holding the weapon at arm's length as I familiarized myself with its weight.

"Don't be holding it like that when you fire." He shook his head and turned, heading for the door. "The kick'll crack your arm at the joint, hurt like bugg'ry."

I adjusted my stance and he nodded.

"Yer in, now," he said. "Be ready for the call."

Patrice's allies planted laughter. Mine planted bombs and guns. All of us were rounded up in the Last March, the great purge, when the mimes swept the city in a pale-faced swarm, eliminating all the trouble-makers one by one, all the feelers and the speakers and the ones who fought back.

The mimes came for us in my room, which was something of a mercy. They could have destroyed The Laughing House and all who resided within, guilty and innocent alike, but the Mimes are not devoid of compassion. Patrice returned from her meeting in a lather, slamming the door and panting. "There are mimes in the hall," she said. "Three of them."

Her cheeks were flushed from running. The smell of greasepaint followed her, seeping in through the door. I heard the familiar squeak of the balloons. Something bobbed past the window, a flash of black and white and red through the gap in the curtains.

"Well..." I said. "Well."

Then I got the gun from its hiding place in the bottom of my wardrobe. Patrice stared, open-mouthed, as I checked the safety was off.

The door swung open. The mime's feet tapped the floorboards as he bobbed in the doorway, hanging from his red balloon. He screwed up his face, twisting knuckles next to his eyes. A grotesque mockery of grief, but it hit me like a slap. I jerked out a few tears before I brought the sleek nose of the Beretta up and squeezed. The Mime had sharp stars drawn over his eyes, the black pigment smudged a little where he'd rubbed at it during his performance. The gun kicked and something went *sput*, sudden and bloody, in the mimes arm. The Mime's face twisted as he bit back a scream.

Patrice sang a hymn, belting out the words from a place deep in her stomach. The second mime bobbed through the door and mimed a wall to use as a barricade. One white-gloved hand curled, fingers held around a non-existent trigger. The other hand twisted the air and the Beretta went spinning, disappearing beneath the bed while I scrambled after it. A third mime entered. He zipped his lips with two fingers. Patrice's voice fell silent. She stared, eyes wide, and tried to force her mouth open. Her lips stretched, warped, but did not open. I fell to my knees, searching, but I couldn't find the gun. Patrice ran for the window and I looked away. I heard the shattering glass. I heard her body hit the street, the impact so soft, so quiet.

They let me see Patrice; a tiny, broken doll surrounded by shattered glass, her hair sticky with pooling blood. I stood over her while the mimes stood guard, floating around me in a diamond formation that left no easy escape. One of them bled from his shoulder, the left arm hanging limp. The western point: he was the weak spot; the method of breaking free. I looked east towards the Leviathan, the great arms spread over the city as the mimes floated upwards with their prisoners. The great beast was wreathed by smoke, a black cloud drifting up from the temples where dissidents and speakers burned for their sins. I watched the smoke, the shadow behind it. We were never going to win. It was all just marking time. "Better to die caged than follow them to the temple."

The mimes cocked their head in unison, their faces blank. Mime blood pattered against the road, soft drops on the bitumen. I weighed my chances; no-one tries running once they're surrounded. They had me cocooned in a wall of mime, but I could break it. I could try.

I turned, meeting the too-large eyes of my captors. "Show me," I said. The mimes cocked their heads the other way. They blinked in unison, fingers steepled. "You've won. I'm not going anywhere. The revolution, the underground; all of them are done. Show me."

And the leader nodded, reaching out. He placed a gloved hand upon my forehead. He showed me what had been, and he showed me the world writ in the Leviathan's image, and he showed me how they'd found me and that I'd always been right. He removed his hand and I knew it all, the bloodshed and the slaughter and the knowledge of my duplicity. The war we couldn't win, no matter who fought it. I saw the endless silence, vast and immeasurable. No whispers, no creaking wind, nothing but the void. I saw the last shining thoughts of Patrice as she fell, a mix of anger and hope and betrayal. I envied them, the mimes, for their abilities with silence.

And then I ran. I pushed west against the chink in their wall, leading with my shoulder and hitting it with my weight. The wounded member of the quartet crumpled and I hit him to make sure, right fist making contact with the paste-white cheek. I pushed past and I ran, and the mimes did not chase me. They didn't really need to. There was nowhere to go; nowhere safe for me to run.

I kept moving until the explosions started, until the last of the Underground fought back. The leviathan loomed against the darkness, its bulk illuminated in fragments as the buildings around it burned. The mimes filled the sky, a gathering shadow against the stars. Everywhere there was screaming, detonations, gunfire. We'd broken the silence, refused to end quietly.

I said Patrice's name. I waited.

The silence would return soon enough.

The Girl In The Next Room Is Crying Again

It's Morley's hotel. I didn't know that when I checked in, when I told the night clerk my name was Mister Cassidy and asked for a room on the top floor. The knowledge came slowly. Slower than it should have, considering.

It's Morley's hotel and Morley's on his way and I no longer have the energy to run.

This isn't much of a room to be dying in. It's cramped and cold, the walls a sickly shade of faded avocado with black spots creeping up from the carpet. The curtain rod is bent, sagging in a wide V between the curtain hooks. The walls are thin and the girl in the next room is crying again. I've been listening to her cry for hours. Twenty-three hours and sixteen minutes. Not the entire time, but most of it.

I know this, I have notes.

She stopped long enough to take a shower this morning, and again to pad down the hall and stop in at the cigarette machine. I can still taste the smoke from Lucky Strikes in the gaps between sniffles. I'm trying to distract myself, reading the Gideon's bible, hungry for sensation. I'm running my finger down the ragged line where someone has torn out the first three pages of Leviticus. It doesn't do much good, and when she upgrades to sobbing I put the book down and pad over to the wall so I can hear a little better. Making contact with the stucco should be sharp, but the hardness gives way to something unpleasant, soft and slick as toad-belly. I want to jerk my hand away, to wipe the misery free, but I don't. I don't.

The sound of her tears is glorious.

I blow my nose to clear it of the death-stink and take a shallow breath.

Morley would tell me I'm wasting my gifts, using them for frivolous voyeurism. I reach out anyway, pushing into her room, but there's too much grief and cigarette smoke to get anything else. I wait, patient, long enough to catch a fresh burst of tears. I can taste each one as it falls, a fizz of salt that melts against the tongue.

Eventually it gets old and I retreat to the bed, lie there unsure of what to do with my hands. The hotel room is sweltering, humid in a way that only Brisbane can manage.

Morley's going to kill me here. The smell of it is everywhere; a faint stink like rotting oranges beneath the bleached scent of hotel sheets. Not strong, not yet, but Morley will come; it's not like he'd delegate a loose end like me, and circumstances argue against death by natural causes. Morley wins by process of elimination.

I'm okay with it, mostly, the dying. I just wish the room was a little cleaner, a little cooler during the nights. I wish the television in the corner worked so I had something else to do while I wait for Morley to show.

• • •

I used to think it was no big deal, the sensing. After all, everyone smells stuff. Everyone tastes things and gets those nervous feelings in their gut, or that twinge across the back of their neck that tells them something's up, the vague foresight of intuition. It was Morley who taught me otherwise, who told me I was special and taught me what else I could do.

He found me rehab. Rehab is full of people like me, people who smell too much and hear too much and taste thoughts or moods hanging in the air; people who just know too damn much about the folks around them, predicting their actions and picking up on thoughts up by osmosis. We get caught up in drinking and popping pills, trying to lock our minds away from the rest of the world. None of it works, not really, so we end up in rehab and go a little crazy from too much close proximity. There's something about smelling each other, about slipping into each other's heads, that makes everything worse. When people like Morley pull us out and offer us a purpose, well, more often than not we take it, no questions asked.

It was Morley who taught me how to shuffle, how to reach into someone's head and change the memory triggers. "It's like the smell of baking bread," he said. "Makes me think of my mother, yeah, but you can use it to trigger anything you want. Shuffle enough of those around, introduce the right memories, and you can rebuild a person any way you want."

Most people are easy to understand once you know how, their very scent a memory trigger that lets you remember their whole life for them. Morley was like that, when we first met. I knew who he was, what he was, right from the outset.

Some people are trickier to understand, a puzzle requiring prolonged study and close proximity, revealing themselves in momentary glimpses that may never form a complete picture. The girl in the next room is one of the latter, so I make up stories about her to fill in the gaps.

My current theories, an overview: she's running away from home; she's running away from her boyfriend; she's haunted; she's been told she has cancer and three days to live. All of these are broad strokes, basic guidelines to work from until my gut tells me I've got something right. I have longer lists written in red pen on hotel stationary, a constructed life jotted down and scrubbed out in haphazard order. I start a new list every hour, accumulating details until sixty minutes have passed.

At one o'clock, just after lunch, I write the following: *Her heart is broken. Her name is Susan and she once loved a man named Kristoff, a tall man with hollow cheeks and the kind of laugh that sounds like a sniffling elephant. The two of them were never happy, not really, but they clung to one another for years because they thought it was necessary. There were no children, not after the miscarriage. She worked in a library; he travelled a lot. It surprised all their friends when she was the one who had an affair, who ended things when she could no longer stand the nights alone. Now she's here, weeping, refusing to be ignored. Weeping because her lover was supposed to come and hasn't. Because he was killed by a drunk driver on his way to meet her. Her lover's name was James. Or Stephen. Or Chris.*

None of this is correct. She doesn't cry like a Susan, and a lover's absence is too convenient, simultaneously too spectacular and too mundane for the depths of the emotion displayed on the far side of my wall.

I fold the paper in half and add it to the pile. I wait for the clock to tick its way around to two and start the process again.

. . .

Morley was right about me, I did need a purpose. His seemed as good as any other, at first. Without him there's nothing left but this room and the girl and the endless waiting for death to arrive.

The Night Clerk shows up just after eleven, knocking on the door to my room and whispering the fake name I gave at the front desk. The Night Clerk smells like clean socks and folded underwear. He's easy to read. His secrets are ordinary, all shame and masturbation. Too ordinary, too easy; I entertain the possibility that they aren't real, just the product of a shuffle designed to keep him safe.

He tells me lies about phone calls and messages left at his desk. He tells me I need to change to another room because they want to do repairs in this one. He pretends this is an expensive hotel, offering service far better than the money I'm paying. We've been doing this for three days now, ever since I arrived. I still haven't seen the Night Clerk, but I know the taste of his presence too well. His lies are like an overripe grape, sour and too soft against the tongue. I spend the hours he's on duty watching the door. Occasionally I sit on the couch that I'm using as a barricade. The Night Clerk's tried to move me three times in the last hour. I refuse to give him the satisfaction of opening the door. The first faint whiff of orange can be traced back to him. He works for Morley, I think. His bland secrets shuffled into place, hiding something darker.

"Mister Cassidy," the Night Clerk says. "We really must get in and clean the room. You must need fresh towels, sir. You must need something."

I tell him I'm fine and listen to him walk away. He goes downstairs to the front desk and whispers something into the phone. He knows I can hear him, so he keeps his voice low.

.   .   .

Three o'clock and it's dark out, my room lit up by the green glow of the neon sign bolted to the exterior wall. The crying keeps me awake. I'm making notes on yellow paper. This time her name is Pamela Watson. She was a detective with the LAPD. She's trying to outrun her problems, although these are unrelated to her job. Or not. Do they connect? Did she kill someone she shouldn't have? She prefers red wine to beer, port to red wine. Dwindling funds reshape her preferences every week that slips by, the tastes of her past giving way to the reality of her bank account. She still has her gun, a thirty-eight automatic. Or would she still have the gun? Wouldn't they take it at the border, or when she tried to catch a plane? Yes, they would have done that. There's no way she could have it here.

When the crying stops she orders pizza. She goes down the hall for a fresh pack of cigarettes. She eats pepperoni on thick crust pizza, the doughy seams bursting with melted cheese. I press my face to the wall and breathe in the scene, the warm cheese and the gunpowder and the man who lies dead in her arms. I hold my breath, savouring it, sorting through the tastes until I find the familiar. I haven't got it right, not yet, but the details are getting closer. I can feel the truth pressing in on me, trying to burrow into my head.

Details are important to a guy with my talents. It's the first thing Morley taught me after he brought me onboard. So much of what we do is guess work, until we find the concrete.

I exhale and reach out, brushing against her mind. I can feel her stomach churning as cheese hits the booze. Her crying stops, replaced by puking. The sour acidic taste of bile seeps through the walls all night.

.   .   .

Morley is there when I wake up, the weight of his presence choking out everything else. Being around Morley is like being caught in an orchard fire, the smell of him as thick and cloying as smoke from green wood. I lean my weight against the couch when Morley knocks. I can hear his breathing, the thick rasp of a big man who has to breathe against his own weight. Morley didn't think of his mother when he smelt baking bread. I don't know that he thought of anything. Morley is a deck of cards still wrapped in cellophane, his history bound tight and impossible to shift. "I've got a job," he says. "Let me in."

I should say no. I should embrace the inevitable.

The weight of habit wins out, responding to the subtle tricks and conditioning Morley's built up over time. I pull the couch away from the door. I unlatch the chain and sit down on the bed. A petty act of rebellion, the only type I've got left. I leave Mister Morley to open his own damn door.

"I've got a job." Morley doesn't sit. He just stands by the bed and looms.

"No."

"I've got a job, and I need a shuffler. You're the best I've got available."

"Can't do it," I tell him. "You know the hotel's history, what it does to my nose."

"I know." Morley's face is bland, devoid of threats.

"I said I was done."

"You did." Morley shifts his weight, twisting his head until his neck cracks. "And if you're done, what happens next?"

I think about the girl, the hotel room, my death.

"Tomorrow night." Morley pulls a letter out of his jacket and hands it over. It feels slimy against my fingers, toad-belly slick like the walls. "I'm bringing you a project."

I say nothing. Morley takes that as a yes. "Nothing fancy,

just a basic rewrite; something that will hold under questioning. We'll call it the last one, if it'll make you feel any better about doing it."

I breathe in and taste the truth buried beneath the lie. It will be the last one, one way or another.

The air tastes like burning toast, the smell of the hotel at rest. I go to sleep against my better judgement. When I sleep the room creeps up on me, the slimy sensation seeping off the walls and flooding my nose. It numbs the sense, shuts them down. Closing my eyes means resigning myself to a day of soiled tissues. I make a note to call the Night Clerk to ensure there's a fresh box waiting for me when the project arrives tomorrow. There's nothing to fear from him, now that Morley's arrived.

Sleeping is easier said than done. The bed sags to the left, just a little, but I notice it. Drifting towards sleep triggers a sensation much like falling. The girl in the next room is crying again, I can smell the port wine in her tears. She has no name, not now, with a project coming. I do not have the energy to work with two sets of details at once. It gets confusing and mistakes are made. Someone is reminded of someone else's golden retriever when they see a tennis ball rolling across the grass; the opening chords of Endless Love remind you of someone else's ex-girlfriend. It's enough to drive a person mad, if you rearrange enough.

She's drinking again, a fresh six-pack of Bud now she's out of wine. God knows where she finds that shit in Brisbane. I can smell her hair, honey-gold and short. I can taste her blue eyes and crooked teeth, her three pairs of jeans that are starting to feel fuzzy whenever she puts them on. She's been living in hotel rooms for too long now, been running away for even longer. She doesn't realise she's in Morley's hotel, stuck next door to one of Morley's boys.

Morley's job weighs heavy on me. It isn't the job I wanted.

At the edge of sleep I start to find details. Her name is Amelia. Amelia Patterson. She's trying to drink away something, but I can't quite smell what. The name is right, and the running; the right backdrop but all the minor details are missing. I can smell the trail stretching back, out of the room and across the oceans. American, certainly; maybe the West Coast is wrong.

I get up, groggy, and step into the hall, bare feet pressing down on the sticky, worn carpet. This is caution being thrown to the wind – the project's already coming. I knock on her door and wait, feeling exposed in the open hall. I can smell the night clerk at his desk, two floors down and safely unaware of the goings on in the hall. I can smell the girl as she stifles tears and looks at the locked door. She doesn't move to open it. "I didn't order anything."

"I'm from next door. I can hear you crying." I turn around and look behind me, just in case there's someone there. "It's keeping me awake. And I can see bits. Things you wouldn't want me to see."

There is movement. She pulls the door open until the chain snaps tight. She's got bloodshot eyes and lips stained cherry pink by the booze.

"Things like what?" she says.

"*Things.*"

She pushes the door shut and takes the chain off. She opens it and lets me in.

"What do I smell like?"

I close my eyes and breathe. "Butter. Melting butter on hot toast."

"You a shuffler?"

There's hope in her voice. It makes me cringe. "I was. I'm giving up. I just wanted you to keep it down."

"Yeah?' she says. "You really think that's possible?"

"No. Not really."

We look at each other, saying nothing. I can feel her grief pressing against my temples. I think of all the stories I've made up about her, about Morley and the project that'll arrive come morning.

"Give me your hand," I tell her. "Whatever it is, I'll take it, or I'll bury it down deep. You don't have to remember, not anymore."

She thinks about it, tearing up. She offers me her hand.

I reach out and touch it and everything is details. It let them wash over me, unconnected to the past. They're better that way. Unconfirmed stories. They give me options the truth never could, triggers waiting for details. They float in the air around me, waiting to be rewoven. I see her mistakes and they're beautiful.

When I wake up I smell nothing, so I blow my nose in the hotel sheets. I press my tongue to my top lip as I breathe in the morning air, tasting the stale bagels and cheap coffee the hotel calls a continental breakfast. The Night Clerk has left food on the threshold of my room, a small box of corn flakes that folds into its own cardboard bowl. I eat, and when I'm done I listen at the wall. It's still there, the smell of oranges left too long in the sun, sharp and acidic and sour. Morley is on the premises. I order my tissues from the Night Clerk and start clearing out my sinuses.

The girl is gone but her grief remains. Her grief is tied to the hotel room now, a faint odor most people will never be able to place. Petty revenge against the Night Clerk, maybe, should people start complaining. Petty revenge is all I've got left. It burns against the fear of what's coming.

I cannot smell her, but the lingering remnants of her presence are like a cold weight against my temples. Morley and the Night Clerk are talking to the Project down in the lobby. The Project is saying unpleasant things about the Night Clerk's hotel. I breathe in and know for certain that one of them will kill me. I can taste it in the air. The project tastes like dark chocolate, bitter-sweet and rich. Greedy to the core. I put my head against the door and breathe deep. The girl is gone. I think she's been gone for hours, possibly even longer. She's as close to safe as she's going to get. She wasn't crying when she left.

This isn't much of a room to be dying in. I wait for Morley's project to walk up the stairs, trying to work out how the inevitable will happen.

The project sits on my bed, causing it to sag. He keeps both feet square on the carpet. He's a big man, moustached, his broad face full of scars. I can smell the history in the old wounds, warm and sweet like caramel. I reach into his head and re-sort them, adjusting the details of their origins: this one caused by a bicycle accident; this one caused by short fight in a bar. The Project has a knife in his pocket, something thin and lean that still smells like blood. He works for Morley, in his old life. I could remake him as anything, anyone, but he'll still work for Morley when I'm done with him.

I breathe in and my head is full of the girl; her smell, her taste, her presence. I reach into the Project's mind and breathe out, sowing the taste of her tears and sorrow over the clustered dendrites of his memory. He curls his fingers into fists, uncurls; marking out the seconds with the tension in his hands. He weeps. He keeps on weeping. Morley sits in the corner of the room and watches, a gun across his lap and a scowl on his face.

It's Morley that will kill me, once he knows what I've done. I reach out and touch the Project's face, running my fingers over the details of his life. He looks at me, suspicious, but trusting in Morley's word. I've never done a good thing before. I'm not sure this qualifies.

I take a deep breath and shuffle, threading in the wrong memories, all the fictions I've made about her while waiting for this moment to come. His new name is Amanda Williamson; he's running from a lover, who is also the law. A policeman named Max with crisp lines in his uniforms, a square jaw full of stubble that's alluring in the right light. Amanda is running, playing blackjack for travel money. She killed her policeman's lover, an aging gambler from the south. Fictions. Half-truths. A chaotic swirl of triggers with no real memories behind them.

The Project is screaming, but that's nothing unusual. I strip his former life away and build another in his place. I give him everything, everything, the stories and the lies and the tickling ghost of not-quite-remembered moments I took from her.

When I'm done the Project won't stop crying, tears streaming down his face. You can taste them in air, thick and bitter with too much salt. Morley stands up to face me, the gun steady in his hands. I see his lips move, tasting the words instead of hearing them. *What did you do?* he says. His face contorts. *Damn you, what did you do?*

I try to answer but the laughter is there, spilling out of

me like blood from an open wound. Morley is screaming but I can't hear the words. He waves the gun and something flashes, something leaps up and bites me right under my ribs. The man on the bed is crying. I'm pretty sure he will never stop. Morley screams at me and his gun flashes again.

And then I'm falling, falling backwards, until I make contact with the dark carpet on the floor. It hurts to breathe, but I smell things. I can still taste everything as blood bubbles over my bottom lip: Morley in the hallway, supporting the project's weight as he runs from the room; the Night Clerk at his desk, thin and pale as chalk; the trail of the girl from the room next door, the long arc of her scent leading out and away into the hot Brisbane streets.

Then everything tastes like oranges. Fresh and juicy and sweet.

Say Zucchini, and Mean It

1.

That summer we used to go searching for the lovesick. Someone'd pick a suburb and we'd bus it out there, a gaggle of us watching the suburbs slip by, killing time. Then we'd split up and go searching, trying to find the weirdest case in the weirdest location. That summer you'd find them everywhere. They'd started calling it an epidemic on the news, and the government was paying a bounty to good Samaritans who called a new case in.

That wasn't why we did it. The money was nice, sure, but we were out there chasing a good story. The whole thing started because Alice found this guy sitting under a jacaranda, back before we knew what was happening. He sat there in his wedding suit, purple flowers covering his head and shoulders like dandruff. Alice said his eyes were dead but his jaw kept working, repeating the same words over and over like a mantra: *I love you. I love you. I love you. I love you.* He'd been left there by his wife, abandoned in the park, when the sickness hit in the middle of the ceremony. No-one knew why she left him. No-one knew what was wrong with him.

We used to love hearing that story, before words like epidemic were thrown around. For a long time we were obsessed with finding one of our own, something even better.

2.

I didn't love Alice, but I wanted to love her. There was something reckless about being in love after seeing the lovesick, and I wanted in. *I love you* was dangerous, the last real taboo we had. Some people embraced it despite the danger. With three simple words you could set yourself free.

3.

Malcolm went away in the second year of the epidemic. Alice and I shared the flat after Malcolm left. We'd spend our afternoons on the couch, Alice strumming bar chords on the acoustic guitar Malcolm's family left behind when they packed up his stuff and had him committed. We didn't have a television, so we'd drink a lot, sing, let our voices boom out against the walls.

On Tuesdays we walked down to the hospital and sat by Malcolm's bed. Alice wore black and sang to him, soft and sweet. I'd stand around and watch, pretending I was somewhere else. The entire ward pulsed with the repetition. A hundred people, maybe more, the same words echoing, over and over: *I love you. I love you. I love you. I love you.*

Sitting there, listening, I realized what epidemic really meant. I recognized it as more than a word they used on the telly.

4.

I hated the ward. It smelt like bleach. Visitors left with tears in their eyes.

5.

One day we stopped to do laundry on the way home, piling our clothes into vast Laundromat dryers. You could fit people in those dryers, sit them in there and tumble them around once you put in the two-fifty to get 'em running. Alice liked the rhythm, the hum of it and the way the clothes rolled over, mixing together as they warmed. We sat on plastic seats watching our clothes spin, Alice's dryer containing a dozen different shades of black. She leaned against my shoulder, her hair tickling my cheek.

I split my washing, colors and whites, a lesson learned the hard way just after I left home. It took twice as long as to finish two loads, but Alice waited around with me. Later, during the rinse-cycle on my white load, I tried to kiss her. That went about as well as it deserved to, given the circumstances.

6.

Before he went away Malcolm worked for the government department putting together pamphlets about the epidemic. He always said avoiding infection was simple: don't say I love you. Not if you meant it, not even if you didn't. Only those three words triggered the disease, leaving you emptied out and vacant while the words spilled out of your mouth. Malcolm's department was responsible for layout and production, but soon moved into finding replacement for those three words. The replacements rarely gained traction among the populace. Malcolm said we didn't like alternatives because the rhythm was always off, that nothing really resonated the same way love did. We needed I love you. We coveted its sound and utility.

Malcolm and Alice were still together the first time we bussed out to find ourselves some lovesick. They sat together in the back seat, holding hands, pretending they were some happy couple, the kind who existed in movies. Malcolm was wearing black gloves with the fingertips cut off; Alice wore an army jacket, dull green and two sizes to big. They still had eight months left then, eight months together before Malcolm disappeared into the ward. They loved each other, I think, but it didn't make them happy.

7.

Alice was the first girl to tell me that love wasn't pretty. "It's all about balance," she said. "No-one ever loves each other in equal amounts."

She said this when we first moved in, before Malcolm went away, when I was still a housemate.

8.

It started with English, so we stole from others in desperation. Sometimes the epidemic spread. Sometimes it did not. No-one knows why *je t'aime* was lost but *wo ai ni* remained safe, but the French were less than pleased when the epidemic reached their shores.

9.

I kissed Alice three weeks after that day in the Laundromat. No, actually, she kissed me. It was a Friday afternoon and she tasted of beer and cigarettes. She put her hand on my shoulder, leaned in to kiss me properly. It caught me by surprise. I hadn't pushed, after that first attempt. I initiated nothing, not really.

"Thanks," I said.

Alice didn't say anything. Then: "I'm just, you know, sick of it."

"Sick of what?"

"I don't know." She kissed me again; pulled back, looked away. Then: "Feeling guilty, I guess."

10.

Some alternatives Malcolm's department suggested in their flyers during the early years of the epidemic: I heart you; I adore you; I am charmed by you; I live for you; zucchini.

That last one was a joke, something Malcom slipped past the editor and never got around to fixing. We tried them all, Alice and I. None were satisfactory replacements.

11.

Actually, I take that back. Alice liked zucchini. She said it's because the words never really mattered, so there's nothing lost with replacing it with something really random. Alice thought we used *love* too freely, for too many things, and that's why the epidemic started. We relied too much on the moment to carry meaning, so love found a way to strike back. "You ever noticed how insincere it is, hearing it repeated like that? You say it once, now, and everyone notices."

I told Alice I zucchini her and felt like a liar.

She said she zucchini me too.

12.

Malcolm loved Alice. He'd told her so, one day, not long after the epidemic started. It came as a surprise to everyone, especially him, but he survived the experience okay.

The second time he said it, when the epidemic actually got him, he should have known better than to try.

13.

Things got awkward when Alice moved back into Malcolm's room. It made sense for her to be there: his room caught the breeze, making it the coolest place to spend summer; his parents had left behind a real bed, with real sheets, when they took him away to the ward. My room remained stifling in summer. I had a sleeping bag thrown over a mattress.

Alice spent the nights crying on Malcolm's bed. I didn't know what to do, so I offered her cups of tea. Three in the morning I'd hear her crying and knock on the door, telling her I'd make tea if she wanted one. Alice came out wearing one of Malcolm's t-shirts. "With honey?" she asked, and I said, "Sure."

"Right then," she'd tell me, and try giving me a wobbly smile. We both pretended she hadn't been crying. Alice wasn't a crier. She drank the tea and went back to bed. Sometimes it stopped the tears, sometimes it didn't.

"You're a good guy," she told me. "I'm glad you're around."

14.

I wasn't a good guy. No-one should be fooled by that. I stopped going with her on Tuesdays when she went to visit Malcolm. She stopped going not long after.

"What's the point?" She said. "He's not getting better."

15.

I walked a lot, getting out. I listened to my sandshoes splotch on the pavement and the street lights ticking in the muggy night air. I fell into a rhythm, started chanting it as I walked, I love you, I love you, but the rhythm never stuck. I was always there, behind the words, forcing them out of my mouth. Sometimes I'd turn a corner and a real case would be there, abandoned on the sidewalk with the words tumbling out. It always made me feel stupid, seeing them like that, but I called the ambulance anyway.

The ambulance drivers told me that three in the morning was a high-traffic period for calls. The same conversation, over and over, every time I called one in. Apparently people said zucchini a lot after midnight.

"It's easy to mean it when you're only half-awake," a blonde ambo said once. "It's easy to forget and fall back on old habits."

16.

I started it, I guess. I said something about feeling guilty, about Malcolm being a friend.

"It's okay," Alice said. "It's not about him anymore. I think, you know, I love you."

I didn't hear her, not really. I panicked a little anyway. "Um. What?"

"I love you," Alice said. "I love you. I love you. I love you."

17.

I don't kid myself about what happened. It had nothing to do with me. Sometimes the person who's there isn't the person you're talking too. Alice isn't the only one who has slipped away like that.

18.

Alice cried the first time we slept together. We both knew she didn't love me. We pretended it was okay, that I was filling in for Malcolm until he came back. Malcolm wasn't coming back. I didn't know what to do about that. "Zucchini," I told her. "Really, zucchini."

I don't think it helped.

19.

The last time I went to the ward there was a nurse working her way down the beds, checking details against a chart and making sure the IVs were still secure. Its how you feed them, the lovesick, how you keep them alive while they repeat themselves. I sat on the edge of Alice's bed, smoothing the wrinkles in her blanket. The nurse paused when she saw me. She was broad-shouldered, built for trouble, tall and formidable. "You family?"

I shook my head. "Just a flatmate."

The nurse checked the chart. "Long time to keep a room open," she said, then she gave me a hard look. "We're only supposed to let family in here."

I stood up, pulled on my jacket. I'm not really much of a fighter when it comes to things like that. The Nurse walked me out, keeping pace to make sure I actually left. "Does it get to you?" I asked. "Working here, listening to all that. Doesn't it do your head in?"

The Nurse shrugged. "I deal with it. You don't notice it, eventually. It all just turns into noise."

We reached the double doors to the ward. She pushed one open, held it there to usher me through. I stood there, looking back, listening to the whispered repetition from the ward. "Don't you think that's kinda sad? Losing a whole word like that?"

"It's just a word," the Nurse said. "There are plenty of others."

"But, *I love you*," I said. "Come on, don't you miss it?"

She shook her head. I tried repeating myself, just in case: "I love you, I love you, I love you."

It didn't take. There was no reason it should, with a woman I didn't know, but it was always worth a try.

"Get out," she said, and I left.

The nurse closed the door behind me.

Clockwork, Patchwork, & Raven

Jackson said she'd been hanging with the Corvidae before he found her, that she was one of those girls that bounced between gangers named Jackdaw6 or Raven8. They'd pumped her full of genemorphs laced with avian DNA, hoping she'd be lucky and avoid the bad reaction. It had already affected her teeth, turning the molars into rotting shards. Her lips were growing hard, thickening into dark cartilage, and I could see the shadow of her organs beneath the bleached skin stretched across her ribcage. Jackson said he found her wandering in the alley behind the crow boy's nest, trying to staunch the fluid seeping from her fresh-plucked eye-socket. He brought her home, patched her up, and turned her over to me for safe-keeping while he went downstairs to work. I stood over her and watched her, letting the hours tick by, and eventually I kissed her.

My kiss didn't wake her, though she stirred a little at my touch. Downside is not a place where fairytales happen, and no-one would mistake me for a handsome prince. It was a clumsy kiss, as you'd expect, but a kiss. A kiss!

When she did not wake I stood, resuming my vigil. I

could feel myself blushing, my right cheek warm. I turned my other cheek towards her, hiding behind the copper mask.

Even now, looking back, I'm still not sure why I did it. It's not as if she was a pretty thing, with her bruises and her missing eye, but there was still some remnant of beauty beneath the blue stitches of Jackson's repair. She was a creature of the Downside streets, all feral promise and rough allure. I didn't love her – that would be unseemly for a half-man like me – but I envied her, desperately, for the blue stitching that held her together and the heart that still beat in her chest. I wished, for just a moment, that Jackson had done the same for me. I could feel the steady flick of that pulse when our lips touched. It was alive; faint, but eager to exist. My own heart ticked on, steady and regular, the soft tick-tock marking a regular beat as it pulped blood through those veins I still possessed.

Jackson wanted to be a hero, I knew that without asking. When I was little, just after he took me in, Jackson used to tell me stories about heroes, about knights and princes and ducks that turned into swans. I would listen to his stories, curled up in bed, crying as the pain of a new graft wracked my chest and shoulder. I had to ignore the sound of the gangs and the crowds that filled the Downside streets, the occasional brawl or gunshot cutting through the din. Jackson would fill my head with heroes, with worlds where heroes still existed. I never believed in his stories, but I always believed in Jackson. It was easier, cleaner, but it was just as dangerous in the end.

The girl slept for three days, sedated and monitored. I spent my nights watching her fight against the painkillers, twisting against the thin sheets in Jackson's cot. I was afraid to move, afraid the grinding cogs in my arms would disturb her bad dreams. I dreamt of kissing her again, dreamt of her waking up and looking on my copper mask and grafted limbs without the inevitable shudder. It was not to be. She woke in the dim light of the third morning, jettisoned from her nightmares with a gurgling scream. She cast about the room with her good eye, looking for something familiar, but all she got was me, and the mangled nubbin of flesh that had been her tongue started making strangled sounds that could have been words. I knelt beside her, putting my good hand on hers, making sure there was contact between her flesh and mine.

"It's okay," I said. "You're safe here."

She struggled and I held her down, the steady tick-tock of my heart frightening her more than the cold grip of my hand. She had a coppery, nervous scent and I saw blood stains on her bandages. Her good eye stared at my face as I leaned in to check the stitches. She waited, trembling and sluggish, still woozy from the barbiturates. I pulled back and limped away. She was scared of me, so scared her fear emerged through the painkiller haze, and I couldn't calm her down.

"You've pulled your stitches," I told her. I couldn't make my voice sound soothing, no matter how hard I tried. "You're bleeding. Wait here, I'll go get Jackson." And I ran, fleeing the bedroom, as she let loose an angry gurgle that should have been a scream.

There was comfort in the clutter of Jackson's workshop downstairs; the overburdened workbenches piled high with bits of clockwork and old tech and equipment we scavenged from the burnt-out hospital on the river. I followed the sound of Jackson's snoring through the cramped maze of junk and spare parts, found him in the overstuffed chair he left by the boiler, soaking up warmth as he slept. He looked old, even for Jackson, the wrinkled features like the grooves of a thumbprint, the wisps of hair hanging limp around his face. I leant over and shook him, letting the metal fingers close over his shoulder. "Jackson," I said. "Jackson, the girl's awake."

He slept, stubbornly, until I placed a cold right hand against his bare forehead. Jackson had built me that arm from scratch, and the one I'd worn before it, and the one before that. Its touch woke him faster than any jostling or loud noise ever could. "Randal?" he said, blinking. His eyes were never good, especially in the dark. I lifted the notebook off his lap and helped him to his feet, setting his journal on a nearby bench while he straightened himself up.

"It's morning, Jackson," I told him. The left side of my mouth twisted into a wry smile. "She's awake and she's pulled some stitches. I think I might have frightened her."

"She'll calm down," he said. "And pulling the stitches won't harm her anymore than she's been harmed." Jackson rubbed his eyes with one hand and smiled his forlorn smile. "How is she?"

"Struggling to speak." I clenched my fist, metal straining against metal. "They took her tongue, Jackson. The crow boys, they cut it right out." It was a mistake to mention the tongue. Jackson nodded, eyes growing distant, and I knew that I'd lost him, that his mind had the association it needed to turn towards to his beloved work. Jackson picked up his notebook, finger tracing the anatomical sketches and blueprints. He was making plans, figuring out a way to replace what was lost. I touched his arm again.

"We should run," I said. "We can. She's awake now. We should run before they come for her."

Jackson looked up and shook his head. "It would kill her," he said. "To move her now, so soon, so soon after..." He shook his head again and sighed. "We need a week. Maybe two. Enough time for her to heal. Then we can leave. Then we can run." His eyes dropped to the notebook as he said it, the blue-and-black plans and the detailed annotations. There was a thump upstairs as she fell out of bed. A loud moan of pain filtering down through the floorboards. I thought of the mangled face, the blue stitching and the scars. Beaten by the Corvidae, Jackson had said. We both knew what would happen when they realised the girl had lived.

"They'll find us before then," I told him.

"I know." My heart beat, tick-tock, tick-tock, as I watched Jackson blink back tears. His face set, trying to hold back a shiver of fear. The Corvidae were bad news; both of us knew that. He put his hand on my shoulder, fingers wrapping across the scars. "But I'm going to take care of her," Jackson said. "She didn't deserve this, Randal."

No-one ever does. Jackson didn't look at me, just tore a page from his notebook and held it out. It was a list of parts, carefully annotated, written in Jackson's sloppy script. I ran down the list, noting the unfamiliar names. They were small parts, tiny. Expensive, too, with our finances.

"I'll take care of her stitches," Jackson said, limping towards the stairs. "It will be okay, Randal. We'll get away before you know it."

I double-checked the locks as I left, nervous about leaving him alone. Most of the time, shopping for Jackson takes effort rather than money. This time he was working small, and that meant parts with names I didn't recognize. Technology; state of the art; the kind with names that read like a secret code. Finding those parts meant someone with black-market contacts. It meant shopping fast and getting off the streets before someone noticed what I was doing. It meant Jackie Pelican.

I went down to the river and found him sitting near the harbor tunnel, hawking cheap tech to Cityside tourists heading home after a day in their favorite kink-house. There was an art to the way Jackie worked, pretending to thumb a ride and then hustling the drivers with cheap promises and stolen tech the moment the car stopped. Pelican always said that anyone stupid enough to stop for a Downsider wearing six jackets as he thumbed a ride was going to be an easy mark for his patter, and it turned out he was right more often than not.

He was cutting a deal when I found him, a lump of layered coats and furs pushing data-chips through the window of a Cityside Lexus. I hung back, out of sight. The Pelican didn't need me interrupting his business, and I knew better than to get in his way. It took him five, maybe six minutes to close the deal. Money changed hands and the Lexus sped off, threading into the tunnel that linked the Downside grime with the towers and gleaming lights of the city. The Pelican stood by the side of the road, shuffling through his bills, then nodded and slipped the cash into the pockets of his second jacket. I lumbered across the concrete, coming up behind him. Pelican heard me coming, recognized the tick and the steady thump of my limp. "Randal," he said, making a wide turn, his small face beaming among the layered jacket collars. I clapped Pelican on the shoulder and the gears in my arm groaned. He feigned a shudder at the noise. "Clockwork was a bad fad, Randy. When are you going to let me fix you up with something a little less retro?"

"I don't have money for your upgrades, Pelican. You know that."

"You could work it off, Randal," Pelican said. "You're a good kid, talented, and you're wasted in Jackson's workshop. I'm sure I could find a job for you."

"I like the workshop," I said. "It's homey."

Pelican rolled his eyes and laughed, the thick layers of coats wobbling, his throat swelling up as his humour boomed out. "Fine," he said. "If you can't be lured away from the aging reprobate, why don't you tell me what the Pelican can do for you? I assume Jackson's sent you on another shopping trip?"

I held out the list and pointed at the items I needed, letting the Pelican study them through the cracked lens of his glasses. He puffed his cheeks out as his read, fleshy jowls ballooning as he chewed on the air. "That's a strange list, Randal. What's Jackson up to?"

"I don't know, but if I had to guess..."

"Yeah?"

I shook my head and shrugged. "If I had to guess, I'd say he's building someone a tongue."

The Pelican's eyes went narrow and his teeth clicked together. He breathed in, hissing. "A tongue for whom?"

He was standing straight now, drawing up to his full height, bulging jowls starting to quiver. I stumbled backwards, putting weight on the bad leg. Jackie didn't move to help me, he just settled back into the seat he kept near his hitching spot. "I don't know," I said. "Some girl he found."

The Pelican whistled through his yellowing teeth. "Jackson and his strays," he said. "Fuck." He closed his eyes and quivered. I knelt down next to him, waited for him to explain, watching the watery eyes that refused to meet mine. I put the clockwork arm on his shoulder, let him feel its weight.

"What do you know, Jackie Pelican?"

The Pelican let out a soft snort, glancing to either side.

"Nothing, kid," he said. "I know nothing. Just be careful, okay?"

He smiled at me, cheeks rosy, and named me a price. I paid it and collected the parts, lugged them home, worrying.

Jackson had the girl awake by the time I made it back, the steady patter of his speech broken by the stilted syllables of a synthesizer linked to a touch pad. I listened to the dead, cold voice as it answered questions, carrying on her half of the conversation. It was raspy, empty. There were better programs available, but Jackson preferred the retro feel of passive inflections and static. I put the supplies down on the nearest workbench and locked the door, double checking all three deadbolts before stepping back. The alleyway outside was empty, dark even during the day, but talking to Pelican had left me feeling anxious and worried about what was coming. I'd stumbled down three or four different alleyways on my way home, backtracking and cutting through side-streets. I wondered how long it would be before I was actually being followed; sooner or later the news that the girl had survived would filter its way to the Corvidae and they'd come looking for her. I contemplated pulling a workbench in front of the door, damn the mess that moving one would make.

"Randal?" Jackson's voice floated down the stairwell. "Randal, is that you?" There was fear in his voice, but he disguised it well.

"It's me." I limped to the stairwell and waved.

"Randal," Jackson said, "Come up and meet our guest." I shook my head and Jackson frowned at me, his thick eyebrows drawing together. I pointed to the lopsided mask, the arm that had frightened her earlier, and Jackson snorted

"Randal," he said, and I lowered my head. I started climbing up the stairs, my right foot thumping on the wood.

Jackson smiled and took my arm as I reached the top, leading me into the room. The girl was still limp, still caught in the numb painkiller haze, she shuddered when she saw my face. Jackson led me over and sat on the corner of the cot. "This is Randal," he said, keeping his voice calm and low. "You'd call him my assistant, I guess. He took care of you during the evenings."

"Hi," I said. I gave her a lopsided grin. "You look like you're healing well."

She was pale now, paler than when I'd left the workshop, and there were bloodstains on her bandages. Jackson had been drugging her, prepping her for more surgery, re-working the lines of blue stitches that held her battered body together. There were sutures on her cheeks that hadn't been there when I left. The girl scratched her hand across the touchpad, letting the computer beside the cot translate the movements into speech. *Thank. You. Randal. My. Name. Is. Rose.*

There was something lucid beneath the drug haze, something aware of where she'd found herself. She studied my face with her good eye, following the lines of steel and scarred skin, suddenly focused on what those scars could mean. "It's an old job," I said. "And I'm too cantankerous a patient for Jackson to replace things or make them pretty. Don't worry; he'll make sure you're still beautiful when he's done."

She smiled at me then, a terrible expression on her broken face, and winced as the smile tugged at the sutures. Jackson slipped a hypodermic into her neck, easing opiates into her bloodstream. I stepped back, giving him room, watching as she went under.

"Sleep now, Miss Rose," Jackson said. "We'll have you up and talking soon." She shook her head, fingers fumbling for the pad, but the drugs hit and she faded. Her hand went limp again.

Jackson stood up and ran his fingers through the pale wisps of his hair, looking pensive as he studied the ruin of her face. "She isn't going to be pretty, Randal. You shouldn't have lied to her."

I turned around and walked towards the stairs.

"She'll be pretty enough," I said. "You'll rebuild her and she'll be pretty enough."

We both knew he planned to install the tongue before we ran away.

We argued after that, Jackson and I. Argued about running, about rescuing the girl, about trying to install a new tongue while we both knew the Corvidae were coming to find us. Jackson won, as always; he's a smart man, and he has arguments aplenty when he needs them.

"We shall stay," he said. "Who would find us, if they looked for her? Who would even consider looking for a girl in a place like this?"

"Pelican knows," I told him. "He knew the moment I asked for the parts. He *knows*, Jackson, and they'll know to ask him. They're looking, Jackson. They're going to come."

Jackson shook his head, his eyes sad. "We are safe enough, Randall. She'll heal before they find us, and there is always the tunnel if she does not. Pelican knows many things, but he does not know about that." He settled down behind his workbench, sitting in the battered hardwood chair with its back stiff and straight like a throne. Jackson, king of clockwork, master of the world he surveyed. I didn't share his faith in the tunnel. We could get out if we used it, yes, but we still had to run. And the tunnel has been here longer than I have, longer than Jackson and his towering piles of junk. He always told me it was a service entrance, built in the days when the workshop was home to grander creations than ours. It wasn't a secret then, and it was barely a secret now.

That night I took a lantern and walked down the dark length of the tunnel. We had used it as a graveyard, a crypt for the gutted husks of grandfather clocks we'd salvaged for parts. The slow tick-tock of my heart echoed against the stones, mocking the dead clock-faces.

"Safe enough," I told myself, and the words echoed off the walls. It took hours to clear a path, to make sure the tunnel was ready if we needed it. I checked the locks and the keys at the far end, just to be sure. I ambled down the narrow corridor. It would be a short sprint, if running was needed, but I'm not built for speed and Jackson was old. My faith in his plan waned as I contemplated the possibilities.

They found us the day after Jackson installed Rose's new tongue.

Jackson and Rose were asleep when it happened. He, lost in a quiet slump beside the cot, she, twisting and turning through another night of medicated slumber. I stood by the doorway, my heart a metronome beat beneath the steady rhythm of Jackson's snoring, and I heard the muffled thump in the workshop downstairs. I thought it might have been an invention, or a pile of Jackson's parts collapsing in the night. Such things weren't unheard of in a workshop such as ours. It wasn't until the second thump, and then the third, that I realized what it was: someone kicking, hammering, trying to batter down our door. I heard the wood give way, the locks bending inwards, the soft crunch of someone walking across the workshop floor.

We had an intruder, and that wasn't a pleasant thought.

I heard the glass face of Jackson's second-favourite clock shattering beneath a heavy fist, and I allowed myself a few seconds to consider the merits of cowardice. It was tempting; I am ill-equipped for stealth, what with my steel-shod limp and the endless tick-tock tick-tock eliminating the possibility of approaching unannounced. Investigation meant a confrontation, facing the intruder down, and I was coward enough that the thought gave me pause.

I picked up Jackson's poker, a cast-iron antique he'd acquired at an auction. I'd scoffed at him when he bought it, claiming it was useless, but it felt comforting to have a weapon in hand. The poker felt solid, weighted for a quick swing should I need to bludgeon a potential thief, and I held it before me as I limped down the stairs and switched on the workshop lights.

There was a Corvidae in the workshop, languid and ready for my approach. He was an angry snarl of a boy, just like the rest of them, black-feather hair, fingers like raptor talons, eyes as smooth and dark as marbles. He stank of carrion, thick and overripe. I raised the poker, holding it like a sword, ready to cave in the boy's skull with its iron head. The Corvidae sneered. "Ya bully dreaming, Tick-Tock. Me-and-I pluck your vitreous; squish-squish, sweet'n'juicy, yum-yum-ha." He cawed then, cackling. He had a crow's laugh, a harsh croak. "Where da patch?"

I charged him, swinging the poker, a futile gesture fuelled by anger and fear. He moved fast, a dash of shadow against the sulphurous yellow light. It didn't take long, no more than three ticks of my heart, and it was over. I saw him move, felt the poker rip free of my hand, then he crashed backwards with his hollow weight bearing me to the floor. I looked up into a wicked grin, grubby talons hovering over my eyes.

"Where da patch?" he croaked. He kept his voice low, all secret whispers. I shook my head. "Gone," I said. "Jackson's gone. He isn't here."

His talons wove an eager pattern in the air as a narrow,

black tongue licked pointed Corvidae teeth. "Where da girl den, Tick-Tock? You hide our pretty-pretty, our little birdy-bird? We want her back, Tick-Tock. Gotta finish what we started."

"She's not hiding." My treacherous voice quavered, just a little, giving away my fear. "She's not here, she ran away."

The Corvidae gave me a harlequin's smile, leaning forwards to run his long tongue across the tender flesh of my good eye. "Tell da patch I came, Tick-Tock. Tell him Rook3 wants 'is dolly back, no matter what." And I nodded, stiff-necked, my eye following the pointed claw dancing a hair's breadth from my pupil. Rook3 laughed, drunk on my fear. He floated to his feet in a flurry of limbs, dancing and spinning his way to the gaping maw of our broken doorway. "Me-and-I be seeing you, Tick-Tock," he said, and then he was gone, nothing more than a caw of laughter on the wind.

I lay on the floor for a long time.

Jackson had shown me his blueprints for my arm and chest, the detailed plans and notes he'd compiled explaining how and why they work. I know that there are three-hundred and fifty-seven cogs and gears in my arm alone. I lay on the ground and listened to my heart, the steady tick-tock that never felt the surge of adrenaline, never sped up when danger loomed. When I flexed my fingers, pondering their movement, I knew that another hundred and twenty cogs came to life. I tried to console myself with this knowledge, telling myself that clocks are works of precision and delicacy, that they do not lend themselves to strength, or violence.

It didn't help.

Jackson unlocked the bedroom door; his feet padded down the stairs. My good arm trembled. Jackson stood next to me, staring at the broken door. "They came," he said.

"Just one." I stood up, busying myself clearing a bench, moving the junk onto the surrounding piles. When I was done I tipped it on its side, pushing it against the doorframe to replace the door. I leant my weight against it, holding it secure. "He's fast and he's angry. I'm sure he'll collect the rest of them."

Jackson clucked his tongue and forced me to sit, fussing with my arm. He checked mechanisms and servos, double-checking to be sure. He always worried when I fell, always wanted to make sure that I hadn't damaged the intricate parts of his creation. "They want her back, Jackson," I told him. "They want us to hand her over, or they'll kill us both. Kill us and eat our eyes."

Jackson bowed his head and kept his attention on the arm. His face pinched, locked into a frown of concentration. "It doesn't matter," he said. "We'll keep her safe, somehow."

"We need to run. Tonight."

Jackson shook his head, closed the casing on my arm. "If they found us, it's too late. They're expecting us to run and she still needs rest, another day or two at least. We need to stay, keep them out somehow. Give her time to heal, then use the tunnel to sneak away."

I looked at the upright bench, thinner and weaker than our stout wooden door. "How?"

"Somehow," Jackson said. He rapped my arm with a sharp knuckle, the soft echo filling the room. "We haven't got a choice here, Randal. We must do the best we can."

I went back to Pelican the next morning. I bought the best security system our money could afford. "Lethal or non-lethal," Pelican asked me.

"Whichever you've got," I told him. "As long as I can walk away with it today and have it installed by nightfall."

He gave me a queer look and a price, and I gave him the money. It took the better part of a day to get the workshop straightened out and the new locks installed, repairing the door and barricading the windows with steel bars and old workbenches I bolted into place. I spent the afternoon installing Pelican's toys: taser banks and motion detectors; thick Kevlar sheets that sat over the doorjamb, securing it against gunfire and battering shoulders; voltage packs that would pass a charge through anything metal that was tampered with on the exterior of the workshop, leaving a claw blackened and the man behind it stunned. Jackson was upstairs while I toiled below; he checked his work on Rose's prosthetic tongue.

I finished the security job after sunset, just in time for the first Corvidae's croaky laughter to echo at the end of our alleyway. Jackson came down as I was making dinner, flinching at the distant laughter outside. "Done," he said, wiping his hands on a rag. His blue, worn overalls stained with patches of rust. "She can talk."

"Can she eat?" I ladled soup into a bowl and pushed it towards him, then filled a second when Jackson nodded. I started limping towards the stairs, bowl on a plastic tray.

"She's probably sleeping," Jackson said. "And she'll be groggy, even if she's not. Make sure she doesn't choke, Randal – she'll need some practice before she's used to swallowing with the prosthetic."

The whole gang arrived while I was climbing the stairs, loud caws and laughter shrill in the alleyway. I ignored them and kept climbing, opened the door to Rose's room. She wasn't sleeping, but her eyes were glassy from Jackson's painkillers. She was insulated by the drugs, able to look into my face without flinching. She seemed numb to the point where even the noise outside was absent. I sat down next to her and she smiled at me, wincing. "Randal," she said. Her new tongue stumbled around the name, blunting the *n*, but I could recognise the word through the awkwardness. "Your name is Randal."

"I brought you food," I said. "Something soft. Soup. Jackson wants you to practice swallowing."

"I can hear birds," she said. Her face turned towards the window, towards the aftermath of sunset lingering behind the skyline. The song of the Corvidae filled the air.

"Nothing to worry about." I tried to look her in the eye. "You should eat."

I held a spoon before her face, the soup steaming and thick. I watched the patchwork plastic and Kevlar move when she opened her mouth, the faint flicker at the base of her throat as Jackson's prosthetic worked with the torn scraps of her real tongue. Jackson was right – it was ugly work, but Rose remained beautiful. I fed her a spoon at a time, using my good hand to guide the spoon. The crow calls grew louder, cutting through the groggy haze. She stopped eating and turned to the window, shuddering.

"It's them." She said. "They... hated me. They told me to leave. Why are they here?"

"No-one likes to lose," I said.

She blinked back tears, remembering. "Why am I here? Why aren't I dead?"

I thought of Jackson, sitting downstairs, working his way through a bowl of soup. "Jackson likes old stories," I told her, and she frowned. "Fairytales and stuff. You needed help and he helped you." I clenched my fist, listening to the gears creak. "He does that, sometimes."

The painkillers kicked in, responding to her stress. She drifted off, unable to fight Jackson's drugs, and I went downstairs to listen to the bird calls. Jackson was by the stove again, hidden in the corner of the workshop. He cradled a half-full bowl of soup in his lap. The Corvidae were right outside now. I turned the lights off, one by one, relying on the shadows to give us some cover.

"She's scared," I said, settling into the stool next to him.

"She's a smart girl," Jackson answered. He lowered his head and stared into the murkiness of the soup, wispy hair falling in front of his face. Something thumped hard against the front door and the charge went off, filling the air with ozone. We listened to something young and birdlike squeal in pain, then the sound of a limping body retreating into the distance. "We should have closed-circuit," Jackson said. "I don't like hearing them without seeing what they're up to." The second thump was more solid, prepared for the shock that followed. The sound echoed across the workshop as the taser's hiss cut through the darkness.

"Pelican didn't have any cameras," I said. "It'd take at least a week to get some in."

Jackson slept in his chair, fitful, flinching with every measured assault against our doorway. I stayed awake, keeping vigil, the poker gripped in the clockwork hand. My slow hand, the hated hand, but it was strong enough to shatter bone if I could land a solid blow. Jackson used to tell me stories about a broken boy who was put back together by kindly elves with a talent for magic and clockwork. He would tell me the boy's arm was magical, that his heart was a wonder in a world where hearts rarely beat, where all too often hearts were lost for no reason. Love was a powerful thing in Jackson's stories. It could conquer armies and rewrite time. It could make the broken whole again.

I passed the time by counting the thumps of Corvidae against the door, the rattle-rattle-buzz of claws against the window bars, the electrified charge sending bodies reeling back with scorched hands and strangled cries. They paced themselves, syncopated the assaults, used the silence as a weapon to keep us on edge. I counted the thumps, one after the other; one bird, two birds, three birds burned. Four birds, five birds, six birds harmed. Occasionally I stood by the doorway, listening to the quiet scuffle of clawed boots against the concrete. Sometimes they were swift and raucous, using the echoes of the alley to their advantage. They filled the air with birdcalls, making it impossible to be sure of their numbers. Other times they were silent, murmurs in the darkness. I figured there were twenty three of them out there, including those who'd been shocked by the taser bank on the door, birds shocked by enough voltage to leave them twitching and stunned until morning. Sometimes I pressed my weight against the door, keeping it steady against the assault.

Around 2 a.m. it all went quiet. I listened to the steps of someone loping up to the doorway, leaning in without touching it. "We know you're in there, Tick-Tock," Rook3 whispered. "Me-and-I hear your heart; tick-tick-tick."

"No-one here but us chickens," I told him, voice cracking. I picked a spot by the door, raising the poker high, just in case. "Bars on the windows and steel plates on the doors. Go bother someone else, little bird."

Rook3 knocked, three sharp raps that echoed on the steel. The air filled with a whiff of ozone and Rook3 screamed, then cawed and cackled as his screams turned to laughter. "Nothing save you from me-and-I, Tick-Tock," he said. "You come out, sun or no-sun, and Rook3 be waiting."

There was no more knocking after that, no more electrical discharge or rattled windows to break the silence. Later, as the sun rose, I peeked through a crack on a second-floor window and watched the Corvidae perched on the fire-escape next door, waiting and watching like an army of twisted shadows. I woke Jackson and pointed. "We're locked in," I said. "It appears they're laying siege."

Cops are an expensive proposition in Downside, but Jackson tried calling them anyway. His first attempt got him a busy signal, the second just the hazy buzz of a scrambler attached to the line. The third call was answered by Rook3's croaking laughter. "Nobody going to help you, Patch. You goin' to die if you don't give me-and-I back da girl." Jackson hung up. His knuckles were pale and his hands trembled, but he drew himself straight as he glared at the door. Defiant, angry, but that wouldn't last. I could see the fear there, lurking behind his eyes.

"We should go," I told him. "Use the tunnel, get out while we can." Jackson didn't answer. He went back to his chair and rocked, his face pinched so tight I could barely see his eyes beneath the press of wrinkles. Small, gentle Jackson, determined to do what was right. "So many of them," he said. "I wasn't expecting there to be so many."

I left him there, huddled against the darkness, and checked on Rose myself.

"I couldn't sleep," Rose told me, fighting against the painkillers. "All the noise, it was like being back there. Like living with them." She was still weak, barely able to lift her head off the pillow, but there was life in her cheeks. She winced with every *s* she used, a sting of pain from the sutures as the tongue touched her teeth. It gave her voice an old lilt, at odds with the face full of bruises and patchwork stitches. So many grafts, so many repairs.

"No-one slept," I said. "Don't worry, they can't hurt you here. We've locked the place up tight, and we've held off worse than this."

Rose pursed her lips and frowned at me, the patchwork

tongue bulging against her cheeks. It was a little too large for her mouth, the mechanism heavy against her jaw. She would never look right with her mouth closed, but at least she could speak.

"How..." She shook her head, trying to dislodge the question, but her hand reached out anyway. The dark nails and fingers withered into claws, hovering over the steel, preparing to stroke it. I pulled away, the cogs grinding.

"Jackson found me when I was a kid," I said. "Beaten, cut up, almost dead. He put me back together, the same as you. Replaced the parts as I grew older so I didn't get lopsided." I raised the arm and looked at it, flexed my fingers and took her withered claw in mine. "He's a good man. Foolish, really, and stubborn, but a good man nonetheless."

Outside there was a loud caw, the fizzing snap of a rock thrown against the windows. Rose flinched. "You never... there are other options," she said. "You could get it replaced."

I shook my head. "Jackson calls it his finest work," I told her. "The arm, the heart, the knee. Replacing them would break his heart."

I stood there until Rose gave in to the painkillers, drifting off into sleep with a frown across her face. I held her hand, studied her scars, wondered how far she could make it. Jackson was wrong; we could move her if we had too. Slowly, using a gurney, with enough drugs to keep her sedated and free of pain. We could run if we had to, but we might not get away. The tunnel could get us out, but they would have someone watching. Just in case we had allies, on the off chance someone heard the noise and could be bothered to investigate. If we were spotted as we left, if they saw us sneaking out...

I went downstairs. Jackson was huddled in his chair, shaking. "They won't stop," Jackson said. "They'll never leave us alone, Randal. They just won't stop."

"Then we run," I told him, and I laid out the plan. Jackson listened, eyes flat, and nodded when I reached the end. I sent him upstairs to get things ready. When I was alone in the workshop I let myself shake, skin crawling against the prosthetics. I tightened my grip on the poker, steel grinding against steel. My heart tick-tocked, slow and steady, heedless of my fear.

The Corvidae left us alone during the day, disappearing into the shadows or lingering in knots of two or three, hanging on the fire escapes like birds on a wire. I spent the afternoon taking practice swings with the poker, trying to get comfortable with its leverage and its weight. Violence is easy to practice: swing, parry, thrust; make use of my longer reach. Don't let them get close enough to use speed against me, try to take them down before they rip me apart with their claws. Jackson watched me, lips drawn, trying not to state the obvious.

"You'll need food," he said. "Sooner or later, you'll run out of food."

"I won't run out of food," I said. "And you'll need it more than I do." I smiled at him, awkward and lopsided. Jackson hugged me and patted my arm.

"It'll be dark soon," I said. "You should get ready."

"Sit," Jackson said, and he waited until I did. He told me a story. "It's easier," he said, in the silence at the end. The shadows inside the workshop were growing longer and darker. "In the stories, it's always easier."

"We should get her ready to move," I said. "You'll need help with the gurney, for the first part at least.

· · ·

This time the bird calls started right on sunset, a whole murder of Corvidae starting their mockery at once. I sent Jackson upstairs with two bowls of soup and a pair of spoons, keeping up appearances in case their spies had an angle to see into the house. He pretended he was weary, stomping as he climbed the stairs. He snuck back down quietly, taking each stair with a graceful limp. The wood didn't squeak beneath him, and perhaps the ruse was pointless at this late hour; the plan would work or it wouldn't, whether we maintained the ruse or not. He nodded at me, eyes shining. We turned out the lights.

"Tick-Tock," Rook3 said, calling through the door. "Hey, Tick-Tock? We-and-I getting bored. We be cracking your cage tonight." I heard the regular chk-chk-chk of the taser discharge, the sharp squeal of nails against the metal bars over the window. "Insulated, Tick-Tock," Rook3 taunted. "Me-and-I saw your little friend, saw the fat little Pelican. Got me what I need to break down your little toys." He knocked on the door again; rap-rap-rap. This time it wasn't followed by a scream.

I heard the door to the tunnel slide shut, the quiet click of a lock settling in place. "Me-and-I eat your eyes tonight, Tick-Tock. Eat your eyes and taste the sweet-meat upstairs, after we gut da patch. He shouldn'a saved her, Tick-Tock." Chk-chk-chk as the taser spluttered, useless, against the claws sliding over the door. Nails on the metal, sharp squeal like a knife to the gut. The sound drew goosebumps from what flesh I still possessed.

I readied the poker and stood next to the door; if I was lucky I could brain one as he came through, crack his head open like a stale egg and be done with it before the others swarmed. Maybe I could frighten the rest of the pack off, make them think we were dangerous, better equipped than they'd suspected. They struggled with the windows and kicked at the doors, insulated against the taser discharge but still struggling to break down the barricade. It would take time, but not a lot. I waited. I waited, and the minutes ticked by. I thought about Jackson and his stories, about Rose and her mangled tongue, the patchwork scars that will cover her body when the stitches are pulled out and she's finally healed for good. Jackson was right, she wouldn't be beautiful, but I was right too. I knew it.

Jackson is in the tunnel now, waiting for his chance to run. I wish that I were with him. I wish that I had kissed Rose, just one more time. I wish so many things.

I can hear the Corvidae outside now, a murder of thugs and runaways, hungry for a fight. They're almost in. It's time. I think about Jackson, about his stories. Outside the Corvidae gather, jangling the windows and kicking the door. Four-and-twenty skinny boys, their flesh twisted by drugs and designer mutagens, black claws ready to rend and tear until I'm nothing but blood and parts. I can hear something hissing, see sparks underneath the doorjamb. I hold my breath, waiting for the inevitable. My heart tick-tocks, measuring out the silence. I repeat the same phrase like a mantra, reminding myself why I'm staying: *Downside isn't a place where fairytales happen.* I hope I'm wrong. I know I'm right.

The front door slides sideways, hinges and locks worn down by the careful application of a blow torch. The first of the Corvidae comes in, a smaller bird with a nervous tick, his caw humming in the back of his throat. "Tick-Tock," Rook3 croons, calling through the open doorway. "We coming to get you Tick-Tock." The smaller bird hasn't noticed me lurking in the darkness; the clockwork arm steady, the poker raised and ready to strike.

I can buy some time. They're going to need it. Jackson isn't fast, and he certainly can't fight, and the gurney will slow him down even if they don't spot him the moment he breaks cover. Downside is not a place where fairytales happen, but maybe just this once we can sneak one by.

The Corvidae scout takes a few steps into the room, hunched over and eager. He sniffs the air, cocks his head to one side. He can hear my heart ticking, low and ominous in the darkness.

"Go," I whisper, "Please Jackson, get away," and I swing the poker down. It bites into the feathered scalp of Rook3's scout, sends him sprawling to the floor in a pile of blood and skewed limbs. My heart beats steadily, no adrenaline can speed it up. Steadily like a clock, dependable and slow. Jackson isn't fast, but he's always been faster than me. I can hear Rook3's keening, the murder of black figures joining his angry scream. They surge, a dark cloud of anger. I think I can hear my pulse, roaring in my ears. I raise the poker. I wait for them. This is not a place for chivalry, but I can pretend I'm a champion. I can stand against the tide, for a few moments at least. I can buy time for Jackson and Rose. I can. She is not a princess, but she deserves this chance. My kiss did not wake her, but she can still be saved. She deserves this. She does. I hope I'm right.

My pulse rattles in my ears as they swarm in, swarm over me, clawing, slashing; Tick-tock. Tick-tock. Tick-tock. Tick-

Nights like this, Sebastian Crow thinks about his first peek, about that quiet moment in Miss Finnegan's classroom when he realized that all he needed to do to find the answers for math test was to scoop them out of Tommy Keel's head. All the answers right there, flitting around like goldfish in a tank, ready to be plucked out of the furious rush of Tommy's thoughts and dropped into the still water of Sebastian's mind.

And he'd done it, easy, simple as the square root of pi, copied down the numbers and handed the paper in, then gone home happy as hell because, just this once, he wasn't going to fail and there weren't no chance that old bitch Finnegan could accuse him of cheating.

Sebastian stayed happy for three whole days, until the tests came back and the discussions began and he stood there crying while a cane came down across his knuckles, only this time Finnegan had it in for him even worse, 'cause she knew he'd cheated but she didn't know how.

They made him retake the test, later, with no-one around, and 'course he failed this time, without Tommy Keel's brain to peek into and find the answers. That's when he figured out fair didn't mean much, and started figuring out how to play his gift to his advantage.

That was then. This is now.

It's the tippy-tail end of a dogs-arse of an evening. Sebastian sits on the platform, waiting for the two-fifteen train, trying very hard not to think about the hundred and fifty grand he just dumped at the Casino across the river. Never mind that half was Morley's cash, just part of the cost of doing business. Sixteen hours of marathon poker, blowing hand after hand on purpose.

"Throwing people off the scent," is the way Morley puts it. Losing big is Morley's idea, and like most of Morley's plans, it's probably the smart call. "Just because you can win every hand," Morley says, "it doesn't mean you should. Poker's all about picking your spots, kid. Easing people in, learning their tells and patterns. You want to lull them into betting big, then make yourself a surgical strike."

And Sebastian nods, willing to go along, 'cause Morley is right and Morley is dangerous and he's seen the image inside Morley's head, the one where there's a meeting between a nine millimetre bullet and the flat stretch of Sebastian's forehead, should Sebastian make the mistake of trying to cross the big man.

Sebastian restrains himself 'cause Morley says it's necessary, but restraint isn't a natural fit. On nights like this, head aching after sixteen hours flushing good hands down the crapper, he feels the need to tug against his leash.

The two-fifteen train arrives a little closer to two-twenty, pulling into the empty station late and opening up its doors. It's a three-car ride, a third the length of the station, and

Sebastian finds himself thanking God that the last car is nearly empty, populated by a scattered handful of people who cluster together in silent knots.

He takes a seat near the front, underneath an unreadable graffiti tag scratched into the window. Watches the overhead lights flicker as the train picks up speed. Seven passengers, not counting Sebastian. Two football jerseys in the seat behind him, a Samoan kid preaching the word of God to four girls, fresh from a club, seated by the rear door. Mercifully empty, given the hour, but still enough that the presence of other people grates against Sebastian's nerves. He hunkers down in his seat, eyeing off the camera, searches his pockets for the half-empty flask of bourbon tucked into his jacket pocket.

The train carriage reeks, a stale scent like old apples that reminds him of school. Tommy Keels name floats up, unbidden, from his memory. It's immediately followed by the memory of the Old Bitch, Finnegan, and the way she'd hated Sebastian for no reason he could tell, not even when he fished around her head after he learned to control his gift.

He closes his eyes and presses his forehead against the window, using his jacket to cover a surreptitious sip from the flask.

Sebastian shouldn't be drinking—Morley says it messes up his gifts, takes the edge off his control—but on nights like these he's found he doesn't really give a fuck.

He was drunk the first time he met with Morley. Drunk and beaten half-to-death, on account of trying to run. Drunk and terrified, eighteen and unable to cope, still struggling with the days he couldn't keep other people's thought's out. Sebastian remembers sitting in Morley's penthouse, down in the heart of Broadbeach. Remembers Morley sitting on the black-leather couch, a fat man in a black suit, all smiles and finger-rings and teeth like a shark.

"You've got a rare gift there," Morley said. "A rare and impressive gift. Given time, it's going to be valuable, the kind of thing that makes you millions, tax-free. The kind of gift that means all kinds of freedom."

And Sebastian sat there, blinking, blood dripping over his right eye. If Morley was perturbed by Sebastian's blood on the carpet, he showed no sign. "The thing about your gift, kid, is you need some refinement. You still think poker is all about playing the game, and that's one of those mistakes that limits things. You empty a man's wallet once and that's the end. He's tapped and you don't go back there. He talks, an you get a reputation."

Morley tipped his bulk forward, hands spread wide. The silver rings glittered under the soft fluorescent light. "I'm going to teach you to fish, kid, and together we're going to make far more than you've ever dreamed of."

And sitting there, injured and groggy on the couch, Sebastian pulled himself together and tried a peek into Morley's brain, just see what he could find beyond the smile and glittering jewellery.

Two days later, when he was finished screaming, Morley sent him down to Melbourne. Sat shotgun at the table while they played a few rounds and Sebastian played poker the way Morley taught him.

Sat there while he folded a full-house, ceding the pot to an opponent working pocket jacks. Hating himself every minute as he grinned and shook the other guy's hand, even knowing he'd make all the money back.

They're barely out of the station when the club girls clatter down the aisle, searching for the route map posted by the door. The trace their journey with fingernails painted the colours of cotton candy, counting down the stations 'til they reach home.

Sebastian closes his eyes and breathes in, catalogues the details as they slip through his thoughts: a blown curfew; a fake ID tucked into the bra strap; flirting with the bouncer to fill in the missing years whenever the laminated paperwork proved too shoddy to pass for real. He opens his eyes and blinks into the harsh light, wishing he could take another slug from the flask, but he knows it's risky to do that too often. The late trains always have guards somewhere, watching through the cameras. They look down on pubic drinking and passengers who rest their feet on the seats.

He's only two seats down from the Football Jerseys, who have been talking about drugs for the last fifteen minutes, bullshitting their way through a list of gang members they know and prison's they've visited to see their friends. Bolstering their self-image through association with petty criminals, unleashing bluster and bravado in an attempt to prove they're men. Loud voices, uncensored, neither of them as drunk as they wish they were and both of them talking crap.

Their thoughts wash up against Sebastian's skull when they spot the girls by the door, the inevitable mix of anger and toxic desire seeping in, slow and insidious; the club-girls so young, all trim and taut, budding breasts and shirts just short enough to hint at more. The Football Jerseys start talking about rape, trading details about who got away with it, the faggots they know who didn't have the guts to go through with it when the opportunity presented itself, and how desperate they'd need to be before they were willing to try.

Overhearing the conversation is enough to make Sebastian want to hurt them. Being privy to their thoughts only makes matters worse. One of them is lying, talking shit and half-afraid of his own monologue. The other is trying to egg himself on, head full of bullshit and lust and confusion, convinced he's got something to prove. Sebastian tries to ignore it, closes his eyes and works to block them out. Experience says that private thoughts don't always lead to action, that fantasies of domination are built from a place of fear.

He tells himself this, but he doesn't believe it. He's seen the internet, watched the news. Sebastian wishes he'd drunk more, wishes he'd taken things slower this week so he didn't have to throw away hand after hand, wishes he could stop beating himself up when there will be another game tomorrow and another the day after.

Wishes he was anywhere but sitting on this train, soaking in all this shit.

Sebastian closes his eyes and thinks about Tommy Keel, 'cause that's how these nights work sometimes. He squeezes his eyes shut and remembers the days before his gift manifested, when Sebastian Crow was just the weird kid and Tommy Keel wasn't; tall for his age, smart for his age, cruel in a way that many children aren't. Tommy Keel was living proof that geeks are bullies, just like everyone else, but teachers believed the smart kids were above all punishment or reproach.

This one time, on school camp, when Tommy Keel walked over to Sebastian, backed up by a bunch of other kids. Tommy Keel with cards in his hand, a whole damn deck, the edges frayed and browning from over-use.

"Hey 'Bastian," Tommy said, "you want to play fifty-two pick-up?"

And Sebastian knew what was coming, without the gift;

knew by the smirk shared by Tommy's friends, but the absence of cruelty in Tommy's broad face.

He tried to avoid it, protested he didn't know how to play and had no desire to learn, but Tommy kept on at him and promised it wouldn't be hard. Egged and cajoled and wheedled until Sebastian gave in, setting himself up for the joke.

Standing there, outside the cabin, a shower of cards flying into his face while the other kids laughed.

The pain starts as a quiet, deep thrum that rattles in time with the click-clack of the train. Sebastian starts to hum under his breath, starts singing the theme song to *Family Ties* before he realises what he's doing. Realises it's 'cause one of the Jersey's looks like Skippy, defines himself by his resemblance to an awkward teenager on an eighties sitcom he's only ever seen on cable. Sebastian can feel the Jersey's anxiety when he hears a snatch of the song, feels a sudden hatred for black curls, glasses and chubby features. Years of teenage frustration welling up as Skippy stares at the club-girls, still thinking of himself as sixteen and mawkish some twenty years after the high-school taunts have ceased.

Crow can sense the club-girls retreating down the aisle, leaving a cloud of sugar-lime perfume in their wakes. The Samoan boy-preacher welcomes them back, wraps them in his gangsta-patois, selling them scripture as best he can. *You gotta accept God, man, otherwise you're just a sucka.* Sebastian can taste the kid's faith, the curious mix of superiority and desperation in his hard sell.

Sebastian's head starts to pound. He puts a hand in his pocket, feels the comforting weight of the bottle. He should have drunk more. Get drunk enough and he doesn't see a damn thing. Stop short and he can't keep a damn thing out, all the thoughts and tastes and memories around him start rattling through his skull. Crow tastes Skippy's desire, a desperate longing that's more need than wanting. The other Jersey is still talking about rape, bullying Skippy with the word. Using it like a club, all blunt force impact. Skippy's squirming in his seat, wondering whether the conversation's crossed a line, telling himself its okay. Just talk. Just being a little edgy.

Sebastian senses the tunnel in the distance, the looming darkness where the camera will miss details. His mind trawls the carriage like a drift-net, snaring thought-fragments and pulling them in. The boy-preacher dreaming of heaven, rising up into the air while the club-girls burn for teasing him. The club-kids thoughts, all hormones and ecstasy, fragile constructs that jitter when he touches their minds. One of them, blonde, a little more sober, aware of every guy not he carriage and the potential to do her harm.

Skippy in his Bronco's jersey; a single word, a single *image*, bouncing round his head. The other Jersey revelling in the power to make his friend uncomfortable, still talking shit and pressing the point home, grinning and confident he's safe as long as Skippy doesn't balk and overcome his discomfort, his habit of letting these things slide because, "they're no big deal, just boys talking shit, he's a nice guy. He wouldn't really do nothing."

Sebastian hates them both, on reflex. Hates everyone in his orbit on a night like this. He closes his eyes and feels the thrum of their thoughts, chaotic and wild, brushing against the drink-worn skein of his defenses.

He figures someone should have a worse night than he is, and starts to go to work.

· · ·

"The first time you play poker," Morley says, "you're all about the cards in the hands. It don't matter what everyone else has, it just matters that your hand is golden, yeah? What you gotta do is play the table, man. Look at the cards on the table and know every play that can come from that, every combination that can trash what you're holding. Once you've got that down, you just play the players. That's where you and yours excel, once you learn the magic of it."

He says this so often Sebastian can't even remember the first time. He just remembers the smile, the way Morley claps his plump hands together.

"Play the man, Crow, and you lose on your terms."

Nights like this, Sebastian reminds himself he's essentially expendable.

It's a truth Morley took great pains to establish, feeding crumbs of truth to his protégé in the weeks Sebastian spent learning. Morley let down his defenses, feigning moments of weakness, letting Sebastian grab memories of other kids, other players.

All of them gifted, able to peek. All of them found and cultivated by Morley, whether its for gambling or something *else*, something that lurks in the big man's brain like a monster's shadow. All of them interchangeable, from Morley's perspective, and all of them dead when they outlived their usefulness.

Sebastian promised himself he'd stay useful. Learned the control and the discipline he needed to follow orders.

And for a while there he convinced himself he was just biding time. That one day he'd figure it out, a way out of Morley's organisation. Convinced himself he wasn't the same kid dumb enough to get caught peeking into a classmates answers, even if Miss Finnegan couldn't explain how it happened from the other side of the class.

Sebastian takes another furtive nip of the bourbon, follows it with a deep breath. Figures, if he times it right, the darkness of the tunnel will cover things and Morley won't find out. He reaches out with his mind, searches for the thoughts of the passengers, sees them floating there, waiting to be scooped up.

It's Skippy that leaves a bad taste in Sebastian's mouth, his fantasies all power-trip with the menace and self-loathing leeched away. A hollow bluff backed up by a hand full of random cards, devoid of threat and meaning. He's shirking away from the dark heart of his own day-dream, telling him anything he does is okay if she enjoys it. Sebastian is almost tempted to tip his hand before they reach the tunnel, holds himself back with a dry swallow of bourbon.

Part of him thinks back to camp, Tommy Keel standing there with cards in his hands. Sebastian turns and smiles at the carriage. He senses the blonde girl's fear, the very sensible unease when faced with a public-drinker with hollow eyes and a jacket that's too heavy for the cool autumn air. Sebastian eases his hammering head by forcing the taste of the bourbon on her, suppresses a smile when she gags and splutters.

The thrum in his head is echoing like a bass drum, loud as a lover's cry, clear as the word of God. Thoughts seeping in from all sides, penetrating his skull like harpoons. He can feel the pain rising, a queasy feeling in his stomach as he takes on more. The net pulls tight around the carriage, pulls everyone close and compact in his mind. He can sense the tunnel ahead, seconds away. He feels heavy, weighted down by the long night and the candy-sour booze.

He pushes deeper, unpacks the dark recesses of memory that surrounds him. Pulls the secrets and the hidden desires together, shuffles them like cards while he listens to the anxiety seeping into the air. Jersey's hunger to hurt people, the blonde girl's fear, the boy-preacher's loathing. All the hidden thoughts and fears, set aside to cope with the fact they're all trapped together in a steel box rolling along a train line.

Sebastian listens to the click-click of the train wheels, looks up into the metal-box camera and smiles. Thoughts whirling in his head, all the memories pain taking shape like a poker deck tingling beneath his fingers.

Sebastian reaches out and gathers them, all the secret thoughts and bad ideas, the things he'd rather leave behind. It's not a plan he wants to play, so he's handing it on to Skippy. He shuffles the thoughts and feelings and fears, holds them as he waits for the tunnel to arrive. Thinks about school and Morley and Tommy Keel, about the sixteen hours at the table when the cards were firing and it didn't mean shit 'cause he had to fold.

The train tunnel swallows them, leaving them in the dark.

Sebastian grins and peeks into Skippy's head.

"Time to play fifty-two pick-up."

Memories of Chalice

I horde my memories like winter apples, for they're precious despite the sour taste of recollection. Among them is my final sale. Or, at least, the last sale that remains to me, in whole or in part, divorced of continuity: I met the client in the Café Damascus, exchanging greetings beneath the dim light. It was summer in Chalice, warm and sweaty. My client hid his face behind a fishing hat and glasses, casting furtive glances towards the shadows for fear of paparazzo. We ordered steak, cola, fries; all this despite the reputation of the Café's fine lamb tagine. This is my last memory, my last fragment, before my fall from grace.

"It's dark here," the client said, hacking at his steak with a blunt knife. I attacked my meal with far less enthusiasm, but that remains part of the job. "Of course," I said, "the Damascus value's privacy."

"Not this place." The client looked up, waved his fork at the ceiling. "Here, in the city."

"Ah." I swabbed a forkful of steak through the juices on my plate, regarded it carefully before placing it in my mouth. I remember feigning enthusiasm for the meal, for the excess it represented. "Yes, the darkness; a curse of the Nexus. Light moves differently here, in the heart of the mountains; time gets tangled in the tines of the great machine, and what is light but a measure of time and space?"

It's an old lie, the cheap trick of a dealer who's caught a client in need of magic; we cultivate such lies as a tool against those too stupid to look for the easy answers, the high cliff walls that rise above our skyscrapers on every side of the city. And it worked on him, my client, my oh-so-famous client. His eyes went wide behind his glasses.

"Are you for real?" he asked me, and I'm sure I replied. I'm sure I said something, that I seized the moment his innocence offered me. It is possible, probable, but the memory of it is gone.

I take note of my surroundings now, of the familiar rows of white houses and the scent of jasmine that lines the street. Familiarity is valuable to me and I find myself returning to these places, over and over, to solidify their details in the recesses of my memory.

Chalice is a deep city, but modern despite its heritage. I stroll the streets of an evening, watching the helicopters launch like a deadly swarm from the rooftop helipads that populate the high city centre. Once I could have named the men who worked in those towers, could have been one of those passengers travelling upwards on the winds.

There's a danger, too, in wandering; a fear of getting lost. I do not recall things with certainty anymore, nor affix fresh details to places without considerable work. Memory is sacred here, in this city built on the trade, but it is far from inviolate and my memories are long since decimated as a consequence of my past.

. . .

It's said that the punishment is easiest to bear if one thinks of it as a story, that the absences lose their sting when reduced to mere lapses in narrative rather than an actual loss. I doubt this, certainly, but a desperate man tries many things and I am nothing if not desperate. My story starts thusly: I was once a man of wealth, and now I am not. I grew up in the great city of Chalice, the city in the Rift and the home of the Nexus; an orphan raised by my uncle's indulgence at his estate built into the cliffs of the North Quarter. I had a cousin, once, though his name and memory are long-since expunged. I was a trader, unparalleled by any who have ever walked the floor of the Great Exchange or worked in the offices above it. This is the tale of my downfall, built from fragments and rumors and what little I retain of the man I once was.

I first stepped into the vast chamber of the Exchange in the early sixties, just as the market boomed with exotic fantasies and ephemeral, drug-fueled flights of fancy. I'd earned the smock just after my birthday, sponsored by my uncle's connections, and I was ready to make my fortune as part of his team. I can remember the nervous air of that first day, my smock fresh and stiff with starch as I was swallowed by the wild throngs that gathered in the central chamber. I like to think I was good at the job, that I fell into the market like a natural.

It's said I started with the mundane, un-extraordinary moments with little of note to mark them. A risky gambit, given the climate, but it was wise. I was attuned to the looming backlash that was spreading across the world; as real life grew wilder among the tumult of rock music, drugs and conflict, the customers longed for something simpler. As memories of sex grew plentiful, the demand for the placid recollection of home and hearth grew exponentially. I traded smart and hard, dreaming of the future; a place in the upper offices where the best of us worked, selling exclusive merchandise to the powerful and wealthy.

On the floor we dealt in quantity, following trends like leaves drifting on a current. I excelled at this, I think, but I had no desire to remain there.

When I first got news that I was leaving the floor I wept with sheer relief. It was my dream to make a name as a broker, and I took to the role as a starving man given bread. I kept my smock snowy and pure, unstreaked by the sweat-stains and dust that marked the pit traders. I no longer dealt with the mass-market commodities; I dealt exclusively in the rare and the unique. My clients, my ever-so-wealthy clients, came to Chalice from around the world and I learned to cater to their varied desires. It was a good life, but it wasn't enough. On the floor I was among the thousands, above it but one of the hundreds. To succeed was not enough. I wanted to be the best.

I cannot remember what my last client sought. I do not know why he sought me out.

The man who changed my life didn't seem to be anything special. He knocked softly, hesitating anew each time knuckle made contact with wood. He slunk into our meeting with fetid air of déjà vu. Our eyes met only once and I saw a flash of recognition in the muddy brown of his gaze.

"Gregor Mustapha, yes?" I said, glancing at my appointment book. The visitor scratched at the fuzzy mustache that set off his sallow face. His trader's smock was grubby and threadbare, and I found myself wondering if it was a forgery or simply recovered from the back of a pauper's closet.

"Mustapha, yes," he said, voice unsteady as he groped for the name in his memory. "I am Mustapha."

He shuffled from foot to foot, holding a leather pouch close to his chest. I waited, but he seemed reluctant to hawk his wares. I sighed.

"What do you want, Mr. Mustapha? I'm a busy man."

Mustapha's tongue flicked over his lips, whetting them quickly. Blunt fingers began to fish around inside his leather pouch, and he pulled free a silver orb of light wrapped in layers of glass. He probed the orb with his fingertips, making sure it was the right one, and then held it forward like an offering.

"Touch it," he said. His breath wheezed out of him.

There's strangeness, in this punishment, in the things I've been allowed to keep. Names unattached to faces; faces fragmented into distinctive features without the mundane details to link them; forgotten moments, ordinary, brought forward and made important by the absence of other recollections.

Sometimes its there as a memento, that first orb Mustapha offered me; dusty glass, archaic design, sitting on my desk during meetings or idle moments as I did paperwork or answered phones. Did I touch it, that first day, when the memory was loaded? I preferred to keep the memories abstract, stored away and filed in boxes and crates.

I don't remember making contact, but I remember the silver luster of its light. I remember Mustapha pushing it forward, hand cupped beneath it. He had whiskers on his cheeks, wispy and pale white.

"What is it?" I asked.

Mustapha took a deep breath.

"It is two hours of swimming," he said. "Swimming with a mermaid."

There are parts of this story that remain an absence, elements that exist as a shape in my memory that cannot be filled with detail. I know, for example, that there was a woman present at the height of my success. I may have loved her, I do not know. I do not recall a name, nor a face, just her presence and the curve of her stomach. Other things: kissing her; the smell of her; dawn's light peeking down from the high cliffs above my home; the soft pang of loss that accompanies that moment.

There is an ache to it, this absence, for it remains linked to other memories like a loaded trigger. Like smells that brings to mind a childhood memory, this woman remains linked with the mermaid. To recall one is to reach for the other and find one's hands empty. I do not know why, I do not know how.

But still, oh, that mermaid and the glorious mystery it represented. The Nexus gives us these gifts sometimes, alien memories and realistic dreams from worlds that few dared imagine. To find one and broker it is the making of a legend: twenty years ago Kladdich Omerhyer sold the memories of a planet, perfectly preserved at the moment of its destruction in a supernova; thirty years before that the legendary Amis Zethal acquired the memories of a phoenix, a burning globe of embers and ash that carried recollections from endless eternities of death and rebirth. We idolize these men, carry the memory of their names across the great floor. They are heroes, men who show us what the Nexus may one day be.

There is fancy to it perhaps, or an element of fate. No-one was entirely sure where either memory came from or if they were even real, but everyone accepts the possibility of their existence. We call it a quirk of the Nexus: the same mechanisms that allowed us to segregate memories for trade gives us glimpses of somewhere else.

I was offered a mermaid. I don't remember what followed between Mustapha and I, but let us pretend that I feigned indifference to the revelation. This isn't memory, after all, merely the story of my life, and I can suspect I did as much, even if it was not so. Two hours of an exotic and realistic memory is a rich find, especially to an ambitious young man, but I remained a professional even so. Let us pretend I let my fingers hover above the orb, mere inches from its surface, and made my way through the usual questions, following the protocol set for such exchanges.

"Is there contact?" I might have asked, and Mustapha would tell me yes.

"Kissing?"

"Yes."

"Any drowning, accidental or intentional?"

And let us pretend also that Mustapha shook his head at this, a smile forming on his narrow features. He would know he's hooked me with that, and he would have known what his orb was worth.

"So what's its origin?" I might have said, for the exotic demands caution from a responsible trader. "What kind of dream? Delusional? Archetypal? R.E.M?"

And Gregor's sharp teeth would have appeared beneath his mustache as he smiled. "It's real. Sane and completely conscious, double-tested to ensure it bares all the meme-pattern of an individual memory. I can provide you with the supporting paperwork, if you wish, or you can have it tested yourself."

I would like to think that I hid my surprise; that was part of my job as a trader. Yet I might have let my fingers drop onto the orb at that, reaching out to live for a moment in the mermaid's embrace. Let it wash over me, as real and tangible as my memories of breakfast, of playing with my cousins, of the first time I fell in love.

Let us pretend I withdrew my hand from the glass and considered Mustapha carefully. It's possible I did. "What kind of money are we talking?"

And here we can stop pretending – there was eagerness in my voice. It's still there now, telling you of this, and regardless of the price Mustapha named for my brokerage, I was about to become infamous.

I held onto the mermaid orb for seven months before an adequate price was found. My career and my fortune were made in one fell swoop. Its contents were bid on by rock stars and actors, by wealthy men who had a taste for the exotic and money to burn. Some tried to offer their own memories in exchange for the mermaid; the wild parties of the Rolling Stones bassist; the years of accumulated knowledge from an English professor of anthropology; a dozen orbs containing the ephemera of forgotten ages that were little more than clever fakes.

The mermaid went to none of them. It was a precious thing, unheard of for centuries, and that made selling it difficult. Buyers didn't have to meet my price, they had to find it.

I brought the orb out for tests, of course. No-one would be foolish enough to bid on such a peculiarity without some assurances, and I was not foolish enough to forbid the seeking of such. The memory was pure, tangible and real. Brokering its sale gave me notoriety, and notoriety was the one true path to wealth in a city such as Chalice.

When I was fifteen my cousin tricked me into drawing upon the memory stored within an orb, stitching it into my own life story like cloth in a quilt. I spent three hours as a soldier with a bullet in his gullet, bleeding and weeping as the chill settled in and the inevitable resolved before me. I'm sure my cousin was punished, but I'm unsure if it was enough.

I pause here, to order my recollections, for what follows is one of the few memories I am certain of. Fame is a thing that comes with privileges, and in Chalice there is but one privilege worth speaking of. I was granted it, after the mermaid, though I was the youngest man to have earned the right. It came, unexpected, and I recall it clearest of all the fuzzy and obfuscated details of my life. They chose my uncle as escort, and he appeared at the doorway to my office. It had been three days since I'd sold the mermaid, for a price grand enough to ransom three princes and their consorts.

He was a small man, my uncle, but he retained the broad shoulders and dark hair that had made him seem large through my childhood. His arrival was heralded by the sour cinnamon grease he used to wax his beard, and the soft clip of his cane against the tiled floor of the hallway. His trader's smock was trimmed with gold when he appeared, the first time I'd ever seen an adornment to the simple garment.

He stood in the centre of my office, leaning against his cane, surveying the surroundings.

"You have done well, Nephew," he said. "I am proud of you."

He smiled at me, teeth yellow and brown beneath his mustache. He tapped the cane against the floor three times to make sure he had my attention.

"Come with me," he said as he turned and walked away, and I followed.

My uncle led me through the narrow halls of the upper level, down the winding staircase that placed us at the southern end of the empty Trade Floor. The Great Exchange was a quiet place at night, once the floor traders had left, and our footsteps echoed as we walked across the hardwood floors. I closed my eyes as we walked, filling in the silence with the familiar hawking voices and the clatter of abacus beads. When I opened my eyes there was nothing but empty desks, the vaulted ceiling and the silver spike of the central column. My step faltered as I realized my uncle was leading me towards the column, towards the copper doorway set into the base. We all knew that door, knew where it led, but few of us ever ventured down there. My uncle did not break stride when I hesitated, simply walked and unlocked the door with a great, golden key.

"Come," he said, but I balked, unable to force my legs to move. My uncle nodded, once, a solemn act that betrayed nothing.

"Come," he said again, and this time I followed. He led me down the stairs, into the bones of the earth, to the place where the Nexus rests.

They say it would take the souls of our greatest poets to adequately describe the Nexus and to capture the intricate dance of its spinning strands of blue light and silver wire. The poet Mahari struggled with its immensity, reveling in the burnished sheen of its copper trunk and likening it to the Yggdrasil of the Norse. Kolchec tried to describe that peculiar quality of light it sheds, silver-pale and lonely, like a ghost under the full moon on a night long forgotten. It was

Lyracov that named the Nexus the Astrograph of Dreams, describing its presence like a fingerprint that will be forever stored upon the wax of our souls. I am a merchant and I have no talent for poetry, so I can only tell you that the great machine stole my breath and made me weep. I stared at the copper base of its trunk, at the shifting web of stars and silver light that stretched out into forever.

Few men have been so close to the Nexus. It remains our greatest privilege, reserved for those who brush against greatness. I stood there for an hour, taking in the slow revolutions, before Uncle touched my shoulder and drew my attention away from the edifice.

"Enough," he said, softly, and led me back to the stairs. "Remember this. Remember that this is what lies at the centre of all your success. It is bigger than you, bigger than all of us, and you must treat it with caution. This one thing, you must remember. It cannot be bought, or sold, or explained. Remember."

And this much, at least, remains to me. This much they could not take away, regardless of my crime.

I do not remember the address of my childhood home. I cannot remember my uncle's name, nor any feature of his face but his beard, his teeth and his rounded cheeks. I do not recall the color of his eyes.

I sometimes wonder if things might have gone differently, had I been content with but a single success. Had I made my name and never seen Mustapha again, simply living on the notoriety of that first momentous sale. I return to the same conclusion – there is no other way, no other path I would have chosen. The only thing that would have stopped me is if

Mustapha had never returned. Even now, remembering so little, I crave the moment of discovery when he came to my office.

Some things cobbled together from rumor and the list of charges at my trail: we sold the memories of an angel floating in the void of space, close enough to the vast expanse of the sun that it could reach out and touch the day-star's boiling plasma; we sold the memory of a twisted dwarf breathing life into his metallic bride and of the sailors who fell in love with the songs of the siren; of the forging of Excalibur by an old god who dwelt at the earth's core; of the coronation of the first Queen of the Americas, prepared to reign immortal and forever from her Washington Throne. Mustapha brought them to me, months or years apart, and I bought every memory he offered, time and again, drawing top dollar for the exotic wares.

I remember so few details of his visits, though these absences, at least, are my own fault; those memories were valuable once, at the height of my notoriety, and I had thought then that there were enough to go around. All I remember now are his hands, large and pale; hands that offered things forward like gifts, jewels of heaven. I remember the pale scar he had on one knuckle, his touch soft despite the callused fingers. Despite our success, Mustapha didn't change; he remained an unkempt man in a dirty smock, perennially stained with an air of shaggy uncertainty.

The Café Damascus is a dingy place, a place for unsuccessful floor traders and those dabbling in the black market. I could have afforded better, as could my client. Why there, of all places? Why did we seek shadows to make our deal?

There's a clue perhaps, though I have not the resources to riddle it out.

.   .   .

I'd predicted its arrival, the ending of our business. The months between Mustapha's visits had grown longer and his prices growing higher, as though challenging me to find a client who'd meet them. The quality of the memories he brought grew sloppy, the details of their origins vague. Then, on that last visit, I could see the strain in his face. Mustapha had never been a healthy man, but this time his features were sallow and his face seemed somehow wrong – like he'd been deprived of sleep for days before his body had been shattered, then rebuilt with sloppy precision. On his last visit this creature, this facsimile of Gregor Mustapha, sat down on the far side of my desk and laid a perfect golden orb before me.

"It is the end of time," he said. "The final moment where the universe breathes its last. It is the end. There will be no more."

I picked up the orb and I can still feel the empty void of the memory singing through me like a choir. "It will sell," I said. "There are men with rare tastes and they will savor this, cherish it."

"No," Mustapha said. "You don't understand. It is the last, the last memory. I can bring you no more."

I was prepared for this, but I feigned surprise. "I understand," I said. "The last. We shall sell it for a kingdom, that you may live off your fortune."

Mustapha's shoulders slumped and he sucked in a quick breath. He'd been preparing for a fight, I could see it in his features, but he didn't have the energy to distrust my response.

I have heard that my fall was borne of jealousy, some misguided desire to destroy the man who made me wealthy.

It's not true. I'm a trader, a broker who deals in the memories of others; what use did I have for jealousy, except as a memory to be sold to those desiring a taste of such emotions? Though I sought Mustapha out, sent men to follow him and sniff out his secrets, I didn't send forth my hounds until he announced the end of our association.

He lived in a bad part of Chalice, in the shadow of the southern cliffs. An aging townhouse my men found on my behalf, following Mustapha home and recording his movements before calling me in. I should not remember what I saw in Mustapha's home, but I do nonetheless. There are some things that cannot be stripped, not even in the name of punishment.

It was a crude place, rudimentary, and bore little sign of the wealth that had filtered its way to Mustapha through my fingers. I brought help, for I have neither talent for skulking or skullduggery, and I remember the hammering heart and sweaty palms that overcame me as I watched my men disable the locks and traps that secured Mustapha's door. I remember the ill feeling that overcame me as I stepped across the threshold, the unbidden recollection of childhood fears associated with darkness and decay. Mustapha's house was filled with the stink of smoldering metal. The upper floors felt much like a mausoleum, the furniture covered in sheets. Our footsteps left tracks in the thin patina of dust.

What I remember clearest is the cellar, and the warped hoop of steel that resembled a tree root. Suspended in this hoop was a tiny replica of the Nexus, small and perfect like a precious jewel, twisting in the darkness like a mangled star. The space between replica and hoop was a void, an absence that ached when gazed upon. And when one gazed into that void ... Well, I have no poet's words to fall back on, but I will say this: within that void lay possibilities, a myriad of worlds no larger than a grain of sand. It was a void full of places that could not be, their existence sewn together by Mustapha's machine.

I killed my own men to prevent the spreading of the secret, neat gunshots in the silence of the cellar. I fed Mustapha, screaming, into the rift of his creation. I watched his coffee-skin turn pale, pearlescent, as his existence unraveled, his body unstitched by the energies that consumed him. I murdered them, covetous of Mustapha's last secrete, and I sought a way of understanding what he had done.

There is a line, they say, between genius and madness, and even now I am not certain of which side Mustapha walked. To tamper with the Nexus is treason enough, but to succeed was unthinkable. In his death I gathered memories, and with his memories I saw obsession; I saw the wealth that went into his strange device, his own personal astrograph opening the door to the memories of the universe. He was a man devoted to research, not wealth, and he'd used me to fund his scholarly pursuits. I learned this much from his memories, but this was not enough to save myself from what would come.

I do not remember bringing ruin down, but it found me nonetheless. Did I try to use Mustapha's device and fail? Was it my fault the memories went bad?

Again I rely on rumor: that first memory, the mermaid, was supposedly sold to a Russian heiress. The daughter of a diplomat who remained fascinated with myth and fairytale. She was found floating in a pool on the French Riviera;

dead by drowning if you believe the press, but there are rumors that her body had grown a layer of glistening scales. A customer who'd acquired joyous recollections of breathing life into a metallic bride was found dead not long after, his blood mixed with a viscous molten silver that caused his heart to rupture. There are others, better and worse, though I suspect I need not go forward. The wealthy and the famous dropping dead as their memories killed them, a little portion of another world bleeding through into our own.

I lived without fear in Chalice. We are a city built on trade, open and unrestricted; we adopted *caveat emptor* as our motto, in spirit if not in practice. We have learned the art of the subtle defense, the threat of censure and withdrawal of the Great Exchange when governments moved against us. There were several men who came for me, armed men in suits who worked for the wealthy and others in black uniforms who claimed they worked for no-one. I survived the attacks with relative ease, secure behind the bastion of influence I'd created.

The ire of the outside world didn't bother me, but it served as a useful tool among the jealous peers who wanted me gone. They needed someone, a scapegoat to blame. I offer no ill-will for this—I would have done the same. I hired additional bodyguards and fortified my home, expecting attack from every quarter.

They came at me in my penthouse, crashing through windows of colored glass that gaped like open wounds. Behind them Chalice stretched out, the burning lights of a thousand windows filling the space between window and the walls of the rift, a patch of darkness near the centre where the Great Exchange lay dormant until dawn. My bodyguards died swiftly, bullets drawing forth short fountains of blood as they made futile attempts to dive for cover.

I was tried by my peers. Two dozen men of Chalice wearing white smocks and grim expressions, all of them nodding as the charges were laid. Lawyers stalked the court-room floors, sneering as they used terms like *dangerous memories* and *potentially volatile product* to describe my crimes. Mustapha's name wasn't mentioned, his death a flyspeck when compared to the threat those stolen, otherworldly memories posed to trade and business.

I was convicted with little opposition. They stripped my memories as a result, stripped them down and destroyed them as dangerous artifacts. It seems so painless, to be stripped of memory, but the things one misses are great. Memories fade with time, even here, but to loose them en-masse is as tangible as the loss of a limb. Yet it is not irreversible, in a city like Chalice. With time and wealth one can rebuild, replacing what is lost with memories stolen from other sources. I had wealth aplenty despite my crimes, and time enough in the aftermath to acquire new stock. Had that been the extent of my punishment I could have survived, could have flourished and formed a new life as a better man than I once was.

They did not simply take the memories that were. They used the Nexus to steel memories that might yet be. Such was the depth of my crime, and the punishment demanded for what I'd done.

A final memory, flawed and incomplete: I'm back in the Café Damascus, the client peering over his glass of cola as I look away and blink. So very young, this client, so very young and eager to buy. He teeters on the knife's edge, ready to purchase. All that remains is finishing my story and naming a price.

"It may not be much of a story, I know; so many things missing, so many moments gone. When times are hard, in a city like this, memories are sold and stories fade. It is the nature of Chalice to treat every story as clay, to adapt it to new memories and replace missing details. This is what you are buying, yes? The chance to reshape your own story as best you can, to draw upon things you need not experience."

The client looks at me through his glasses, keeping his face still. "The price," he says, nodding at the sack that's sitting at my side. "How much?"

And as I open my mouth to name the price, to feel that momentary rush when he agrees to what's asked, my client disappears and I remember nothing. His choice is gone, his transaction a mystery. Even the few scant dollars in my bank account give little indication of whether he swallowed the hook or not. They are all like this, my memories of clients, from those I once knew well to those met in the weeks after my fall. All that remains are patches, glimpses of the moment where we cut the deal. The rush of the sale is absent, each client's agreement a blank space in my mind.

I breathe deep, focusing on the memory. The client's face is fuzzy, indistinct: a chin; a twitch of the eye; the plump lower lip. I can no longer remember his name. "The price," he says, "how much?" I remember the sensation of my mouth splitting open, the words ready to speak. I open my lips, gaping, trying to mimic the sensation.

And all that remains is absence. Everything else is gone.

They've been together long enough for this to become ritual: Deanna Sable in the clawfoot bath, head resting against the curve of the tub, her fingers coiled around a Stuyvescent smoked down to the filter; Kirk seated at the door, bare-chested and nursing his third beer, drawing what comfort he can from the proximity to the cracked tiles. Watching one another, half a smile shared between them, looking for new ways to fill the idle silence.

"My dad was twelve years older than mum." Deanna breathes against her cigarette, stubs it against the side of the bath. "Her parents lined it up. Country towns, you know? Thank God my mum got out eventually."

She opens one eye, checks that Kirk is listening. He takes a swig of beer, nods once. "Never heard much from my dad, either way," he said. "Christmas cards. Socks on my birthday."

Deanna furrows her brow, points to the half-empty cigarette pack. "Light me up," she says.

"Come on."

"I'm in the bath, fucker. Light me a damn cigarette."

Kirk sighs. Puts down the beer and crawls across the tile, frees the cigarette and a lighter from Deanna's half-full pack. He doesn't remember how it started, not really. Not the ritual, not the things that came after. He enjoys the opportunity to watch the pale and naked woman soaking in the tub, the swirling eddies of steam caught in the dying afternoon light. Deanna lying there with her eyes closed, bruise-colored lips pursing a little as she brings the cigarette to her mouth and lets him apply the flame, breasts emerging from the water as she breathes against it.

"So after she left my dad, mum married a sloth," she says. "Not a lazy fucker like you, but an honest to God sloth. Three toes and no desire to move, which makes the toes the main point of difference between him and you, I guess."

"I can cut off a few toes, if it helps," Kirk says.

"Shut up," Deanna says. "I'm trying to tell you something important."

Kirk shuts up and Deanna takes a deep breathe, but there's no more story coming. He's disrupted her train of thought. The heat of the bath makes her lazy, even as the silence wears on her nerves.

"You did that on purpose," she says.

"Not at all."

"You did."

Kirk shrugs.

And the sun sets and the bathroom shadows grow longer, forcing Deanna to light a candle, and as Kirk starts in on his fifth beer, she opens her eyes and says, "fine, you tell me a story, then."

Kirk tries not to flinch. "Nah," he says. "I'm all out of stories."

And Deanna flicks stray droplets at him; dips the

fingertips of her left hand into the bath, reloading for a second attack. "Fucker," she says. "Just tell me a story."

And Kirk nods and clears his throat, five beers down and ponderous, acknowledging the inevitable. Maybe, this time, it won't be so bad. Maybe, this time, he can fix some of the damage.

He coughs. Splutters. Clears his throat.

"Okay," he says, "okay, so. Once upon a time…"

If Kirk is certain of anything, it's this: he doesn't love Deanna Sable.

He knows this because he needs truths to cling too, because lies just make things worse and confuse him even more. He's learned to embrace the certainties, to take comfort in their presence. So this is a truth he lives by: he doesn't love Deanna Sable.

Another truth, reasonably consistent: they live in an old house down in the Pendulum, just left of the bridge that takes you across the river. The house is an ugly thing trying to be beautiful, its walls stripped bare and left half-painted, several of its doors removed and never replaced. Rumour has it the former owner was killed doing the renovation, some kind of accident with a nail gun or paint thinner. Maybe they aren't even rumours, just stories Kirk made up to sate Deanna's appetite, filling in the empty minutes while she soaked in the tub.

The stories became real when he wasn't paying attention.

Another truth: they get cheap rent in exchange for not complaining about the absent doors, or the yard that resembles the aftermath of a battle.

A truth: Deanna smokes too much.

Another: Kirk drinks too much and, occasionally, when past the line, he consents to tell her stories despite his promise to stop.

Sometimes the stories are true. More often, they make themselves true when Kirk isn't looking. He isn't sure when it happens, maybe when he's asleep.

There is no room for maybe. Not given the circumstances.

A truth: Kirk isn't sure if he should stop telling stories. He isn't even sure which ones are dangerous anymore. He isn't sure, now that they've started, if ending them would have consequences.

But he doesn't love Deanna Sable. Not the version of her that slips into the bath, not the version of her that slipped away a hundred stories ago.

He doesn't love Deanna Sable.

God, it would be so much worse if he did.

Tonight's story. "Once upon a time, after the war was over," he says, "the ghost-boy and the dead girl walked down the promenade looking for flowers."

Deanna's eyes peer over the edge of the tub. "Am I the dead girl?"

"No."

"But you're the ghost-boy, right?"

"No."

"So not a real story then?"

Kirk takes a deep breath. Some Tuesdays, too many of them, he catches glimpses of the Deanna he used to know and it hurts.

He doesn't answer the question. Just ploughs ahead. "Neither of them could tell you what species of flower they were after, although both had one in mind. The flower caught in the ghost-boy's memory was white and broad-petaled and possessed a heart the colour of butter, and he clung to that description despite the fact he could barely remember the taste of butter or the smell of it or anything but it's name. The dead girl's flower was pink and curled around itself, resembling an undelivered kiss of unimagined sweetness.

"But there were no more flowers, not since the war. And everywhere they went and everyone they asked, the answer was the same: do not be so foolish as to want something you do not have. Forget your flowers and return to the graves from whence you came.

"But the ghost-boy and the dead girl were made of sterner stuff, and so they kept on walking, always going forwards regardless of the heat or the cold or the hail or the rain."

On Tuesday mornings Kirk wakes up and takes their beat-up old hatchback down to his latest job. He's drives on autopilot, letting his body follow what feels like a routine, but every Tuesday it's a new job and Kirk is forced to figure out what he's actually meant to be doing. Once he worked in an office, making photocopies of some documents he didn't really understand. Once he worked in a 7-Eleven, and he stole a dozen packs of cigarettes and some beer before he left. Once he worked as a foreman. Once he found himself at an abandoned zoo, just south of Long Neck, and couldn't work out what he was meant to be doing.

In the real world he worked a register job. Scanning groceries, bagging them, sending the customers home happy. That's the last job he remembers getting, the last time he actually knew how to get where he was going.

But he'd hated that job, hated it more than he hated snakes or horror movies or his little brother's irritating laugh, and when Deanna asked for a story one night he'd told her a fairy tale where he finally got to quit and ride off in the sunset. It wasn't the first story, although it was early on. Maybe it started things. Maybe it did not. All he knows is that he didn't work a register after that, and he's not entirely sure when everything shifted.

On Tuesday evenings he comes home and they go for walk, strolling the length of the Pendulum district in the hazy twilight. Kirk doesn't say anything about his day at work. Deanna doesn't ask. Instead she strolls beside him, black parasol erect and held above her, eyeing every streetlight as if its soft illumination could burn her pale skin.

Kirk opens the last beer and tosses the six-pack wrapper towards the bathroom bin. It falls short, just shy of the sink, and he doesn't leave the door to fix it. Deanna watches, her face turned golden by the candlelight. He opens his beer and drinks.

"It was the dead girl's idea to find flowers again," he says. "She remembered them from the days before the war, before the tanks and the bayonets and the soldiers and the grenades. In the dim recesses of her memory she kept a catalogue of names she would recite like an incantation: primroses, violets, snapdragons, daisies, roses. pansies, baby's breath. She could recite them all, but they were just names. She couldn't remember what each flower looked like, what it smelt like, how it could be recognised. The names refused to link with any memory she had of what it was like to experience a flower, to be in its presence.

"The ghost-boy didn't care for flowers, although he felt something sharp and eager inside him when the dead girl suggested they start their search, and that feeling left him with a faint sense of longing that he couldn't quite explain to the other ghosts in their small town. He'd elected, thus far, not to haunt a person or a place or a thing, but as their question continued and the longing grew stronger he wondered if, perhaps, he was destined to haunt whatever flower they ended up finding."

He stops and lights a cigarette, sucking against the filter. When Deanna Sable gives him a look, he lights another and rests it against the side of the tub. Waits for her to dry damp fingers and claim the spare cigarette as her own.

"They search for years," he says. "For so long that somewhere along the way, even they forget what they're really looking for. The image of the flower they carry around inside their heads fades a little, the memory wearing away like a well-handled photograph beginning to deteriorate. Finally they end up searching, searching for its own sake, driven to keep looking by a mission they can articulate without understanding: we are looking for the flowers, have you seen any? Do you mind if we look around anyway?"

Kirk comes home from a Tuesday spent welding on the twenty-third floor of a construction site down by the Necks. He closes the door behind him and leans against it, holding it closed with his bodyweight. The house is dark and quiet and the exposed bones of the kitchen wall seem oddly frightening in the shadows. Deanna potters about in the back room, folding laundry, smoking. The back of Kirk's neck is sunburnt. He still feels unsteady after so many hours spent aloft, trusting in instincts that aren't really his own. His hands are shaking. He wants to drink.

He holds it together, concentrates on breathing. Inhale. Exhale. Inhale. Exhale.

By the time Deanna emerges from the back room, awake, alert, Kirk is ready to pretend everything is normal. She says hello and he kisses her on the cheek and one of them makes coffee, black with two sugars, that they share on the back deck.

"It's a nice evening tonight," Deanna says. *"We should go for a walk."*

"I don't feel like walking. Lets stay in."

"I've gotta go out anyway," she says. *"I'm running out of cigarettes."*

Kirk seizes her packet, hears the soft rattle of its contents. "You got enough for tonight," he says. "We can go out in the morning."

"In daylight?" Deanna's presses one hand against the curved O of her lips. It's an insincere mockery of shock. "Surely you jest."

"People go out in daylight."

"They do," Deanna says. "I do not."

"Then I'll go," Kirk says. "You can stay here and wait. It's only fucking daylight, Dee. I don't see the big deal."

There is nothing insincere about Deanna's shock now. She purses her lips, stays silent, watches Kirk with tear-shine eyes.

"I wanted us to go for a walk," she says, very quietly. "I didn't think that was a big deal."

She stands up and leaves the balcony, collecting her parasol from the stand in the hall. For a moment she lingers beside the front door. "Kirk?"

Kirk breathes in. Breathes out. "Yeah?"

"I'm going for a walk," she says. "You want anything from the shops?"

He doesn't answer. Doesn't even breathe. Just sits there, waiting, until he hears her footsteps descending and the soft squeak of the garden gate alerting him she's gone.

There is no truth in the guilt he feels. There is no truth in the anger.

He does not love Deanna Sable.

If he doesn't, it's possible he can leave behind the nightmare. If he doesn't love Deanna Sable, there is still some hope of escape.

. . .

There is silence in the bathroom. Water drips for the faucet, plinks into the water with a tiny splash.

"Well," Deanna says, "do they find the flower?"

Kirk picks up one of the beer bottles, rattles it without expectation. "Who knows? By the time they find something that might be a flower, they've got no idea how to identify it. They could be cooing over a discarded hubcap, or a dead mouse, or some weeds they found by the river. You spend long enough looking for something and the thing itself ceases to be important. It's the looking that matters."

Deanna stares. It's dark in the bathroom now, except for her flickering candles, and her stare takes on a particular gravity in the absence of bright light. "Arsehole," she says, "we're not in a fucking kung-fu flick. Stow the philosophy and give it a real ending."

Kirk sets his jaw. "Or?"

She frowns. "Or?"

"What happens if I don't."

It takes time for the frown to disappear. "Just give it an ending, asshole," she says. "Tell me a happy story for once, okay?"

Deanna walks with a black parasol regardless of the hour or the season. Kirk is left to squire her, his arm threaded through her arm, as they stroll along the length of the Pendulum Bridge and turn left when they reach the far bank. His skin crawls where it makes contact with Deanna's cold flesh. He wonders, not for the first time, whether she really remembers anything that happens from Tuesday to Tuesday. Whether some part of her remembers the world that was, rather than the reflection of whatever story he's told most recently.

Sometimes they reach intersections, and he wait there for Deanna to make a choice. Minutes turn into hours, sometimes, while he refuses to give her a cue. The times they do not he worries that he still has some unseen tell, that she's reading his intentions from cues he doesn't know he's giving her.

Sometimes they sit in the park, underneath one of the ancient gum trees that still exists amid the pines. Deanna perches on a swing, rocking back-and-forth. He sits on the grass and watches her.

"Hey," he says, "tell me a story?"

Deanna says nothing.

"Come on, Dee. You can do this," he says.

She can't. Won't. Not until they're home, until she's in the bath. The one bubble of time in the whole deem week where things can return to normal.

There are no happy endings anymore. Of this, he's almost certain. Every attempt to make things better has ended up making things worse. Still, she asked, and even this Deanna is enough to play on his sympathies, to convince him that an ending is necessary even if it's dangerous.

"They travel the world looking for flowers, and they see some extraordinary things," he says. "There are mountains in Africa where there are no more flowers, but the clouds cling to the rising cliffs and the rainbows that are caught on the eddying mist are so beautiful that they become heartbreaking. They uncover deserts in Australia that refuse to bloom, even after rain, yet all manner of strange creature emerges from the sands to greet them as they pass through. There are cursed gardens in Paris where too much blood has been spilt, and fallow gardens in parts of Russia where the locals treat the ghost-boy and the dead girl with suspicion, and yet in both places there are broken fragments of beauty, places where nature has reasserted its dominance over the man-made confines and unleashed something warped and dark and powerful.

"And slowly, as they uncover these moments of beauty, they remember things. The ghost boy remembers what it's like to have flesh, to feel solid and know the weight of a body that breathes and pumps blood and does as one bids it. The dead girl feels the warmth of the sun and knows the joy of that warmth spreading through her, eager and insistent as life itself, wanting to spread into every finger and toe and nail and strand of hair. She remembers what it's like to breathe and desire and want, really want, more than anything.

"They remember things no war can take away. They remember each other's names. They remember how to feel, what to feel, when to feel it.

"And sometimes these memories hurt, because there is no light without shadow to give it contrast, and sometimes the memories make them cry, but for the most part they feel alive and they learn to delight in one another's company.

"And it's true they never find the flower, because there are no more flowers to find."

Again, the dripping faucet. The soft exhalation of Deanna's breath. The short squeak of flesh against the copper tub as she adjust her position in the tub.

"That's what you've got?"

"That's what I've got," Kirk says.

"You're calling that a happy ending?

"Take it or leave it."

She pushes her way free of the water, standing there in a bath that now rises to the middle of her thighs. She is pale and beautiful and glorious in the candle light. She reaches for a towel and works it back-and-forth along her shoulders.

"You sure I'm not the dead girl?"

He hesitates. He holds his breath.

"No," he says. "You're not."

And Deanna Sable chews on that while she finishes drying herself. He doesn't love her, he knows that, but there are so many ways he can change that. One story, one goddamn story, and he can slip away with her. He can disappear into the cracks, the little changes that occur between one story and the next.

And once again, he resists the urge. He tells himself its necessary. Someone has to endure. Someone has to remember.

"So," he says, "what do you think?"

Deanna's pale face breaks into a wary smile. "I'll take it," she says. "I guess it's happy enough."

The bath ends. It's time for bed.

This, too, has become part of the ritual: Deana Sable pulling on a bath robe, Kirk collecting his empty beer bottles and putting them in the bin. She walks past him, making her way to their bedroom, and he takes a moment to notice the sway in her step. Her fingers and toes are pruned from so long in the bathwater, but she lights a fresh cigarette and smokes as she walks, the smell lingering in her wake like a trail for the lost to follow. Kirk stands at the bathroom doorway and breathes the cigarette smoke in. She wants him to follow her. He wants to follow. If he didn't feel so absent, if he could just be certain, if the clarity that comes with ritual didn't disappear so quickly once they left behind the steam and the mildewed tile.

He wants to follow, to believe she's still the Deanna he once knew. To make believe long enough to sustain him from Tuesday to Tuesday, from story to story until he finds one that works. To get through the minutes and hours that used to follow, the end of the ritual that was started by baths and stories.

And instead he sits there, waiting, wondering. Trusting the one place he knows to be true, the fulcrum from which his stories upset the world. He sits in the darkness and imagines the moments stretching out, seconds stretched to breaking point like an ancient rubber band.

He doesn't love Deanna Sable.

He repeats that, over and over, as he thinks about standing, about following her out into the world that reshapes itself after ever tale.

Inside an Egg, Inside a Duck

I hear you're dead, Sebastian. I hear they tracked to Korea, snuck a curse past your defenses and left you to rot in a hotel room. I hear you jumped, rather than watch yourself decay. Sixteen floors, hard concrete, splat. The kind of death that makes a good story, and stories have always been better than truths in this business we engage in.

Better than truth, in so many ways, but it still doesn't make them *true*. And since all I have are stories, whispers and rumors, I choose to believe you live. I choose to believe I should still report in, just as you instructed me.

I am still your monster, Sebastian. Loyal until the end. That much has not changed, not yet.

It's morning in Surfers Paradise and I'm drinking coffee at the cafe at the end of the mall, the one that looks over the beach and the McDonalds and the small strip of road between concrete and sand. It's early, and a couple of surfers jog back from the water with boards under their arms, wet hair hanging into their eyes. An older couple—seventy or eighty, easily—are jogging along the beach track wearing pristine, white t-shirts and florescent yellow jogging shorts. An ibis picks at a garbage bin, hauling free cold fries.

The garbage stinks. Surfers stinks. There are three bronze surf-boards planted into the ground, pretending to be some kind of sculpture. There is sea-salt in the air, and urine, and the wet stink of rotting garbage. I say this without fear of Diesel's people tracking me, should they intercept this letter. I will be on the move tomorrow, out of the country by the time this is sent. In this, Sebastian, you have taught me well. Always keep moving, you said.

I have lost track of Alba, in my travels. Alba, who made you smile. Alba, who brought Diesel and his thugs down on us after we left the Yakuza witch alive.

Alba, who warned me to take care of my heart, not knowing how funny that was.

I still remember the first time you brought her home, a hedge-witch you met at a party. How she occupied our small kitchen, one hip against the counter, waiting for you to make the coffee. Her dark, messy hair. Her steel-capped boots. The faded, much-worn *Young Lovers* t-shirt with its photograph of two pretty boys making out, hands threaded through one-another's Mohawks.

I knew very little about the band—that they were local, punk, and mostly queer—and you didn't know them at all. We were too old by a couple of years, too far removed from the scene. She was proud of that shirt, God knows why. You were ignoring her, so I told her that I liked it. That made Alba scowl a little less. She could, just barely, tolerate a compliment.

She didn't know what to make of me, there in your

apartment. Didn't know what to make of us, when you get right down to it.

I remember Alba's cheekbones and her smile and her skinny frame, so lean I could make out her ribs when she dove on you later and her shirt rode up to reveal the sharp lines of her hips.

I retreated to my room. You took her to yours. She emerged, the next morning, while you were still sleeping. Hovered in the kitchen while I fried eggs and bacon in the sole frying pan we had that wasn't yet dirty. She used the stove-top to light her cigarette.

"So," she said. "You and 'Bastion?"

"Partners," I told her, "but not the kind you're thinking."

"What kind, then?"

"Depends on the day."

I pushed the food around the pan and pretended the smell of grease didn't bother me. We kept paper plates on top of the refrigerator. I took one, loaded it with half the bacon and a single, sunny-side egg already slick with oily fat. "You want this?"

She nodded, slowly, behind her cigarette. Told me it had been two days since she'd eaten. She came to see you for food, I think, as much as the other thing.

It became habit, after that. Giving her things. Listening. Filling in the gaps between you and her. I never did explain, exactly, what we did to earn our money. She never inquired, was smart enough to know that it wasn't something to talk about. Instead, we talked about you. You and her, together. We spent money on things that would make you both happy: jackets; tattoos; piercings; stockings.

Things that would make life easier, as the two of you fell into each other's orbit.

• • •

I took precautions with my heart long before Alba's warning. It was the first thing I did when I started this job.

In fairy-tales, a man who wants to protect his heart from enemies would hide it inside an egg, then hide the egg inside a duck, which in turn is hidden in the depths of a well. The well would then be hidden in a remote and abandoned castle, and everyone would forget the castle's name and the particular mountain range in which it lay.

I have no idea if people do this, on your side of the border between science and magic, but it seemed a reasonable precaution even without access to a warlock. And modern technology made it possible, with far less reliance on water fowl. I paid doctors to numb certain bio-mechanical responses. I took drugs that kept me even-tempered and my emotions deeply submerged. I ceased to feel that thrill when I found myself in the same room as a woman I felt affection for. I did not wonder what it would be like to sleep with every new acquaintance, not even in the fleeting moments when I realized, often later than I should, that I found someone attractive.

I took precautions, Sebastian, because I am a cautious person. You thought it was strange, I know that, but I knew I couldn't trust my heart and took steps to protect us both.

Alba never belonged in our world. The two of you fought over foolish, silly things. The correct pronunciation of benevolent (she was right), and several times over the ways Schenectady should be pronounced (you were both wrong). You fought over who had used whose towel after showering, and what you both wanted for dinner. She asked me, once, how I endured you, and I told her The Business kept us together, gave us something to focus on when the arguments were ready to spill over into a full-blown fight.

This was during the Keating job. Right before Calcutta. You and I were doing extractions that year, removing valuable assets from situations they no longer wanted to be involved with. Eliminating interferences, occult and mundane, impeding in the business of international firms. We were freelance, for hire, willing to go in with guns blazing and our adrenaline running hot. We sent you in to talk to the suits, to sell them on our services with your good looks and your expensive suits and your severe, confident smile.

We sent me in to run the mission, trusted me to make smart tactical decisions and pull the trigger when it was necessary instead of convenient.

We were good, Sebastian. Very good. We should have been better than this.

You used the same smile on Alba, when you wanted to win your arguments. You used the same smile to bring her on-board, when you thought it was necessary.

You met Diesel in a bar somewhere in Barcelona, making contact during the period when we were supposed to be laying low.

You arranged for Diesel and I to meet a few weeks later, in a small Hong Kong bar down by the docks. Another breach of protocol, but Diesel wanted the meeting. He didn't like the idea of going into business without knowing the other half of your team. He was a big guy. Cheekbones like a Mongol raider. He kept his dark hair short and neat, wore a series of rings on the fingers of his right hand designed to ward off evil magic. We were surrounded by his men, although he tried to hide that part. They sat at nearby tables; at the counter; by the door. They tried to look surreptitious, and failed. They wore their guns wrong. Sheathed knives in places that were obvious, so long as you knew what to look for.

If Diesel cared, he didn't show it. "I have a proposition for you," he said. "I'd like you and your partner to come work for me, exclusively, at a rate considerably higher than you're making as freelance operatives."

"Okay," I said. "That's interesting."

"It's more than interesting," Diesel said, and then he named a number.

It was a good number, Sebastian. I understand why you bit. But I told him I needed to think about it. Told him *that* 'cause there's no percentage in saying no to a guy like Diesel straight off. Not when he makes you an offer, surrounded by all of his boys.

I left Hong Kong three hours later, took a direct flight into St Petersburg. Spent sixteen hours there before relocating, renting a room at the Hotel Wein down the street from the Wiener Riesenrad. I'd always liked Vienna, with its river and its big wheel and its endless pictures of Mozart. When my three days were up, I was eating custard strudel in a cafe beside my hotel. Diesel and his men walked in, spread through the place like a virus.

"Well," he said, "do you have an answer?"

He didn't mention my attempts to flee. Just sat and waited, patiently, for me to give an answer.

I knew I wasn't leaving alive if I turned him down, so I gave him the one he wanted.

I asked Alba, once, what people saw in you, Sebastian.

"Power," she said. "It's not just the money, it's the whole damn package. He talks a good game. He gets things done. There's no doubt he'll achieve what he promises"

I asked her what they saw in me. Why she'd claimed me as a friend.

"You?" she said. "You're a goddamn monster who does whatever he's asked. It's like you don't actually give a damn about anyone, except for 'Bastion."

"And you," I said, sincerely.

"I guess."

She didn't look convinced.

Diesel sent us a list of names, intel, and a timeline for each job on the list. Some of those times where generous. Some were extraordinarily tight. You argued in favor of doing them fast, getting them over with and riding off into the sunset. "This is the big score, man," you said. "We do this, we cash our checks, and I'll go live on a beach with Alba, just the two of us, you know?"

Alba. Every time you used her name, I knew that we were screwed. She was under your skin, like heroin. You were convinced, Sebastian, that this was a good thing. I'd seen you do it often enough to know the warning signs.

There were flowers in our apartment that month. Daffodils and buttercups and pristine, tiny daisies. They appeared on ledges and window sills, gathered together and placed in glasses of water, and the both of us assumed it was Alba at work, trying some new technique to pick a fight with you. You'd stopped fighting about the stupid shit while preparing for the job. She had to get creative, if she wanted your attention.

And it worked. You hated the flowers, for all that they were pretty. You roared at her and she roared back. You made up, as you always did, with a loud squall of passion emanating from your bedroom.

You slept heavily, in the aftermath. Alba emerged in your

jacket and a pair of threadbare jeans. She sat in the second couch and lit one of her cigarettes. "Whatever you're being hired to do," she said, "I don't think the two of you should do it."

"Your boyfriend is the brains of this job. Tell him it needs to be stopped."

"He might be the brains, but you're the reasonable one."

"If he listened to me, I wouldn't be living here."

"If he listened to you," she said, "I might be."

We never met Diesel in the same place twice. He traveled, city to city, no base of operations. His business expanding globally as he sought new spheres of influence, no regular dwelling to imprint upon that could be used as a weapon.

He'd established himself by embracing witchcraft earlier than his rivals, using curses and wards against the local families wherever he set up shop. One of his witches was responsible for eliminating half the New York Dons, did the same against the Irish families in Boston when he started out. His organization had footholds throughout the Asia-Pacific, holding their own against the Yakuza and various Chinese tongs. He recruited as he went, found useful tools. Diesel was a man who valued talent, and deployed it to his advantage.

The first job went smooth - a witch doctor in Guatemala. Two weeks' surveillance and a clean, simple hit. A few weeks of laying low before we're home and Alba's there to see you, Sebastian, there to whisper things into your ear and yell about the time we spent on the road. I suggested moving out, getting my own place. You insisted I stay. It made planning the next hit easier, you said, and you liked having me close by.

The second job was a full-fledged witch in Sydney, a thick-set woman who worked out of a new age store, telling fortunes with the tarot and the reading of people's palm lines. You wondered what she might have done to incur the wrath of Diesel, but everyone has a past. Everyone has secrets they'd rather not get out.

The third job went wrong before we were done with the scouting. The witch was a migrant working dates for a company operating out of Berkley. A Japanese witch, although I guess they have their own signifier if you speak Japanese. It would be easy to find that out, on the net, but there are limits to the time I can spend online without leaving a footprint Diesel can follow. Today, I sought out rumors about you, and what went down in Seoul. The correct term will have to wait. We will look it up, one day.

Diesel's notes on the job associated the witch with the local branch of the Yakuza, said she was involved in some underground wars where they'd won territory in won Seattle. There were bodyguards stationed around her house. Thickset men with no sign of a neck, pacing back and forth. Unfriendly bulges beneath their suits where they hid handguns, or worse, from sight.

Security working the house was good. Better than we were used to. They made us as we observed the site, doubled-down on their manpower in the space of an hour. Going in guns blazing would have resulted in casualties, and we didn't have enough people to con our way through.

If we were smart, we would have walked away. Forgot about Diesel's money.

Instead, you said, "we need an in," and I didn't argue.

Then, you said, "I have an idea."

I should have spoken up.

I didn't want to be a monster, but I acknowledge it was necessary. A monster could do what needed to be doing. A man would falter, let his heart dictate his actions. I couldn't afford that, not in our partnership. You were always smarter, Sebastian, by far. You always knew more, made greater connections. You had the ambition to do more, do better.

You had the ideas and I executed. I did what was necessary to get the job done. That was the advantage I brought to the partnership, me and my training and my inert, leaden heart. Good for nothing but the process of pumping blood through my body. Incapable of feeling or desiring or love.

I thought I had done so well, with my heart. I thought I had kept it safe.

We found Alba hustling pool in a pub a few blocks from our flat. You were fighting, that week, split up over some imagined problem that neither of you truly remembered. You both liked to hold a grudge. You both liked to believe that all the blame went anywhere but yourself.

It was the first time I'd seen her outside of your orbit. The first time I caught a glimpse of what her life was like outside of the Sebastian and Alba pairing. She seemed happier, before she noticed us. Before you crossed the dark room and whispered in her ear. Sent her over to me, in the darkened booth, while you went to go get some beers. She sat down on the opposite side of the table, eyes wary as she studied me, tried to figure out my presence at what she assumed was an apology.

"It's not what you think," I told her. "We need your help with a job."

"Babe," she said, "I don't even know what you and Sebastian do. Why in hell do you think I can help?"

"It's not my idea," I said. "I think you should say no."

You re-appeared with the beers, before I could tell her

more. You explained your plan, what you wanted. You convinced her to come on board.

You were always good at that, swaying people to your point of view. I was against it, from the start. She was a tactical risk far greater than the advantages she brought to the operation. But you convinced me, Sebastian, and then you convinced her. You made us a team and we wanted it to work, even though it wasn't smart.

We would send her in, innocent as we could. No malice in her heart. Give her a new identity that would bypass the wards, let her smile and her pretty face bypass the armed security.

I don't love, Sebastian, but that doesn't stop me from knowing the difference between right and wrong.

I went to Alba, the night before the job. Went to her room in the Hilton where we'd put her up under a fake name, one belonging to a black-market trader who dealt in the occult. Alba in a black suit, a briefcase under one arm. Alba with the short, sleek haircut that cost two hundred and thirty dollars. Alba with her crooked smile, when she answered the door and found me there.

"You shouldn't do this," I told her. "Pull out. Jump on a plane. Forget you ever saw me, and sure as hell forget Sebastian."

Alba shook her head. "I'm a big girl," she said. "I can make my own decisions."

"Not about this," I said. "Not without knowing everything you're getting into."

She put her palm against my cheek. Kissed me against the other.

"I don't do what you guys do," she said, "but I've been around. I know some magic."

"It's not a question of magic," I said.

Her next kiss brushed my lips, and I felt something inside my chest for the first time since I started the job. "I said yes. I'm in. We don't need to talk it over."

I'd taken precautions against all this, tried to minimize my exposure. Thought I'd done a good job, even though I know the danger of making such assumptions.

There's no such thing as perfect armor. There's no such thing as an impossible target, if you've got someone dedicated enough to find their way in and hit it.

I used to think, in the dead of night about the girls I once thought I loved, the girls I desired before the operations. Before I closed my heart to better do the job I'd find myself doing. These are the memories that would keep me awake when sleep was just a memory.

Now I just think of Alba. How it felt to have her close to me.

I lay awake in the unfamiliar hotel bed and feel the unsteady, irregular heartbeat that feels so wrong in my chest.

We sent Alba in, briefcase, suit, and all. She went with three armed bodyguards, just to sell the illusion. You and I stayed outside, Sabastian, one of us on either side of the complex. Alba's briefcase had the sigils you would use to start a counter spell, strip down the target's defenses and give me an opening. I could handle everything else, getting in without the guards seeing us, executing the witch before anyone knew. You'd rigged the plan, Sebastian, and you'd rigged the plan to work. You swore it, and I went along, despite the twitch in my gut.

It went wrong so fast, when Alba switched sides. When

she sold us out to the Yakuza witch and left the protections intact. When you and I went for the break-and-enter and triggered all the wards and alarms in the place, bringing bodyguards and warding spirits and Yakuza thugs out of the woodwork.

"Abort," you said, into my ear. "Get the hell out."

"Alba still in there," I told you. "She's in there with the target."

You told me she was the reason everything had gone wrong. You repeated the order to leave, to clear out and go to ground.

I should have listened to you, Sebastian. We could have re-grouped and planned a new attack, lived up to our obligations like the professionals we were. Instead I went in, shedding blood, leaving bodies. I fought my way towards the center with rescue on my mind, and a need to keep her safe coiled up like a serpent inside me.

You always said each job was just a stepping stone to better things. You always thought about what came next, the things you were going to do once you left the work behind.

I never had that Sebastian. I fell into this job 'cause I had a talent, because it was all I had. I stayed with it, throughout our partnership, 'cause I didn't think there was anything better for me out there. I didn't believe in love. I made myself incapable of it. What I had was work and a partner to watch my back. A place to live and enough food and a job that took me places. I saw the world and I didn't care. I killed targets and took the money.

I thought about being the best of the best, Sebastian. That's all I ever wanted for us.

I didn't know how to protect myself when I started wanting something else.

• • •

The first safe-house we fell back to was located in Osaka. I got there over two hours late and you were already gone. Maybe you'd augured who betrayed us. Maybe you simply figured it out faster than me. That was how things usually worked, when it came to people. You pulled out, professional to the end, and I'd gone in messy and I'd pulled Alba out, like an idiot on a crusade.

I was, in that moment, an amateur, Sebastian. I don't blame you for being gone.

She kissed me again, that night in the safe house. She pulled me to her and made my heart beat, and for once in my life I was happy for that. I let myself love her and we made love in the small bed, listening to the rain and the soft whine of aircraft taking off in the distance. The safe-house was going to be safe-enough for that. No-one knew we had it except you and me, Sebastian. You and me and Alba, once I brought her there. Once I let my guard down and drifted off to sleep, her head against my chest and my lips still tingling from her kiss.

It didn't feel like a betrayal, Sebastian. I'm not sure I'm built to know how betrayal feels.

She was crying, when I woke up. Real tears. Fake tears. I'll never be sure. She told me Diesel and his boys were coming. Told me she'd had no choice, cut a deal between him and the Yaks after the job went wrong. That you and me were surplus, the price of doing business. She gave me a bag and my gun and a ticket. Told me to run. To keep running, to get out.

I pointed the gun at her, Sebastian, once the truth sank into my thick skull. I pointed the gun at her and willed myself to pull the trigger, to get some payback for you and for me. To meet betrayal with the only language I've ever known that truly allows me to speak.

She's still alive, Sebastian. Maybe that's a mistake.

• • •

Tomorrow, I leave the Gold Coast behind. Get the hell out of Australia. I'll find another city, another country, another place. I keep moving because there's no safe places left for me, not until Diesel and his boys finally track me down and do whatever they're going to do to keep their new-found peace from shattering.

But I am good at hiding, Sebastian. I am good at becoming someone else. I am good at avoiding the same mistakes, once I have made them and endured the consequences.

Tomorrow there will be a new city. A new city in a new country, on a different continent. I will run faster than Diesel can track me, further than the yakuza and their tattooed witch can reach. I will run until the memories are faded and distant, and then I will start over.

I will take a new name. I will hide my heart again.

I owe it to you, Sebastian, and this time I will do it right. I will hide my heart as it should be: inside an egg, inside a duck, inside a well in an abandoned castle in a place where no-one goes. I will hide it and forget exactly where it has been hidden, so no-one, not even I, will know when to find it.

I can do that, Sebastian. I can become what I was, before you brought her into our lives. Before things went wrong. Before the stories circulated about you and Seoul and the plague curse they slammed through your defenses. I can become that monster once more. I can go and find Alba, face her again. I can take up a gun and point it at her and do what should have been done.

I can face her again, Sebastian. I can be cold and heartless. Two bullets to the chest. Two bullets to the head. Anoint her with holy water before I leave the corpse. I've done it before, will do it again.

I will be your monster again, Sebastian. Because it has to

be better than this.

I will be your monster. I'll swear it and cross my heart, for as long as I still have one.

<h1 style="text-align:center">Visitors</h1>

1.

I found Chilli the morning after Visitation G-27, the one that rolled down the main drag of Surfers Paradise and took a right hook on Orchid Ave, spitting fire and making a mess of the stores selling tourist t-shirts and the giant neon guitar marking the location of our local Hard Rock Café.

It started easy. G-27 wasn't big, only fifty-odd feet long when you stretched him out from tail to snout. That made him a dwarf compared to the high-rise blocks that lined the strip, a nuisance who brought in a storm and pissed off the tourists who still believed it didn't rain in Queensland. Nothing important about him at all, but G-27 registered on Davan's equipment, and that meant Davan needed readings once the rampage was done.

I got up at five in the morning and trudging down the beach, following the line of Attuned surfers with boards under their arms and wetsuits unzipped in reckless disregard for the cold. Crazy bastards, the lot of them. I shivered the entire way down to the waterfront, wrapped up in my leather jacket, nodding at a few familiar faces I spotted among the pack. Good surf was one of the inevitable aftermaths of a visitation, the tides overridden by the weight and bulk pushing through the water when the Visitor finally returned to the sea. Some of them had been Attuned long enough to know what me and Davan did, so they tended to wait for one of us to show before they hit water.

I'm not a surfer. The monster waves did nothing for me. I stood by the shore and took readings. Radiation levels, seismic activity, the usual run of data. Davan had sensor-nests at five different points around Surfers Paradise, another seventy running down the coastline in both directions. He was the brains of the operation. I did the grunt work, poking through the flotsam that washed up on the shore and double-checking the data fed in via the network.

The division of labour was part of how we worked. I found Chilli because readings were my job.

I guess, somehow, it makes what happened my fault.

2.

Normals don't quite get what it's like, living as one of the Attuned, not until they slip over the edge. Davan always used cartoons as a metaphor when he explained it in lectures; the Attuned could see that extra animation cell layered over the real world that no-one else could see, an extra cell full of small landscape changes and the occasional giant monster. Take that cell away and nothing has changed. Davan built up this entire bit around the metaphor, putting together a power-point that featured a cartoon dinosaur overlaid on a photograph of our street. He played it for laughs, a way of deflecting the obvious criticism of his work.

Davan's never seen a Visitor. He's as Normal as you get.

They still ask him to lecture, now more than ever, but the cartoon dinosaur bit is gone and they make him wear a suit and tie. No-one sees anything funny about his research anymore.

3.

Chilli Attuned about five hours before we met. At the time there were only two dozen or so people in Surfer's Paradise who saw the same landscape as me—the churned up sand and the scorch marks running down the street—and she'd joined the ranks more recently than most.

I found her in the same place most newly-Attuned end up, huddled against the edge of the boardwalk where the Mall spilled out onto the sand. Chilli pressed her back against the remnants of those three modern-art pillars designed to look like elongated surf-boards; a Visitor had taken a bite out of them during a rampage two years back, transforming them into shattered fibre-glass stubs with jagged tooth marks pointing at the sky.

Chilli had bleached hair and a surfer's tan. She stared at the ocean with the wide-eyed look I'd gotten used to seeing in the newly Attuned. "They shouldn't be there," she said, pointing at the waves. "A storm like that, no way it could throw up waves like this."

I nodded a couple of times and set up Davan's computer, networking it into the local node for the seismometer array Davan had running the entire way down the coastline. The laptop beeped, green lines oscillating across the screen. Chilli's glare moved from the beach to me, demanding a response. Fucked if I know why I gave her one, because I didn't normally mess with the new blood. There were a couple of minutes to kill. "You're not crazy," I said. "No matter what it feels like, you're not."

"No?" She didn't sound confident, exactly, but her voice stayed steady. I recognised that, the solid determination to cope, no matter how weird things got. I respected it.

"I'm guessing that you heard it last night," I said. "All the roaring and the stomping? The tremor-lines-in-a-glass-of-water bit they do that dinosaur film?"

Chilli nodded. The heel of her hand rubbed away a tear as it formed in her right eye. I sat down next to her, cradled the Geiger counter in my lap. "The first time is always the worst."

The counter ticked, registering the usual residual radiation we'd come to expect from a small Visitation. I recorded the numbers on a PDA, e-mailed them through to Davan. Chilli just stared at me, her eyes hard. Platitudes weren't going to cut it.

"Listen," I said, "do you want the good news or the bad news?"

"There's good news?" Chilli tittered, surfing right along the lip of hysteria and wondering whether it was time to paddle for it and ride the wave.

"Sure," I said. "The average Visitor creates a minor tsunami every time it walks across the ocean floor, and Queensland is still years away from getting the kind of Visitations you see in Tokyo or Los Angeles. Ours are mostly bluster and special effects; they can savage a few power-lines and smash a few windows, but they're harmless enough if you play it safe. Just don't go out and about when they do their thing."

Chilli's shoulders sagged. "I'm not entirely sure how this is good news."

"You're a surfer," I said, nodding to the Malibu sitting at her feet. "Everyone else has the common sense to head inland after their first few Visitations, but a Kaiju kicks the surf into high-gear. You've got, maybe, fifty Attuned surfers spread across the city, half of them clustered in the knot around Surfers so they can make use of days like this. That gives you pretty good odds of getting some quality surf without a crowd on the day a Visitor rolls through."

Chilli blinked. Her eyes were startling, cloud-grey and keen beneath the smudge of dry tears.

"What's the bad news?" she said.

"You're Attuned," I said. "Congratulations. You've now entered the world of random monster attacks that most people can't see. Get used to losing your power every couple of weeks, avoiding the major roads and highways when you're travelling, and getting weird looks from the forty-three percent of Australians who think it's either a mass prank or the onset of hysteria."

"Forty-three percent?"

"There was a poll," I said. "Last month, *A Current Affair*. Nothing official, but it matches with the kind of spread I've experienced first hand."

I tried to give her an encouraging smile. Chilli stared at the water for a long time. It was like she was trying to will it flat, quelling the waves. One hand kneaded the concrete with a steady movement, slowly grinding her knuckles down. My PDA buzzed, a message from Davan asking for more data.

I stood up. "Look, if you want to, you know, throw up or panic or something, that's cool. Most people do, the first time they find out."

Chilli nodded. Then she stood and picked up the Malibu. Pale blue and lavender, covered with hibiscus. It didn't suit her.

"I think I need a drink," she said. "Then you can explain that again. Slow. So I can understand it."

My PDA buzzed three times, angry and impatient.

"Sure," I said, tapping the screen. "I mean, I've gotta get some readings, but I've got beer and bourbon at my place if you want it. You can even talk to Davan; this shit's his specialty."

"You think he'll explain it better?"

I shook my head. "You won't understand a damn word he says, but it'll make you feel like someone's got a handle on things. He does a great job of sounding impressive if you let him start talking about his theories. Just avoid the slang or he'll go a little mental."

Chilli laughed. "There's slang?"

"Kaiju," I said. "Japanese for *strange beast*. Davan thinks it's poor taste to use it, since they migrated to other countries a couple of decades ago."

4.

Davan used to have this theory. Actually, Davan used to have lots of theories. He was a man of theories; it came with the territory when you worked in research. But he had this one theory, the important theory, which said there was something big and unknown lurking under the Australian desert. He obsessed about it, and he'd bang on about it at parties if you gave him enough beer. "It was one, big inland sea," he'd tell me. "One big, fucking inland sea; all loaded up with idealized resonances and so full of potential that it's ready to burst. Think about it, Toby: all those stories about giant rainbow snakes and bunyips in the outback? It's not like they're accidents. It's not like someone just made them up. The Visitors always come from the ocean, but it makes sense there's something lingering out there, under the places the water used to be, trying to get back to the surface."

He had data to support the theory too. Hours and hours of recordings, ghost sounds and measurements on his computer equipment, graphs that charted the rise in white-noise levels and minute changes in Richter scale activity. I never pretended that I understood the data, but I always told people that I trusted Davan. He was a smart guy, and he had a good gut for research. "I'm telling you, Toby, there's something out there," Davan said, time and again. "And if I could find some way to prove it, some data that made sense, I'd almost swear the buried bastard was singing."

He'd always say the last bit like an accusation. Davan wanted to be Attuned, but something in his head that just refused to click over, to pick up on the Visitors and the wreckage they caused. It's a flaw, in a Visitation researcher, and it irked him that I couldn't confirm his theory. Davan used me as a lightning rod, the guy that could see the things he couldn't. I got a place to live and a job to pay the bills. He got someone he could drag out into the Outback and tell him which way he should be pointing his equipment.

Every time we went out there it was exactly the same. I'd stand still, listening, ear cocked to the sky. I'd travelled through the Outback on my own not long after I started seeing monsters, years before Davan and I hooked up. There *was* something singing out there, and it scared the shit out of me. Sometimes the roar of the song would rattle in my ears for days after we got home.

"Did you get it?" Davan would ask me. "Do you know where we should look?"

"Forget it," I'd tell him, the same lie every time. "There's nothing out here but red dust and heat. The Visitors are a coastal thing; they come through with the storms."

Davan didn't respect the Visitors, but I did. I'd lived with them for a long time, and some of them weren't worth poking in the name of science, no matter how much his university paid me.

5.

Davan met Chilli thirty minutes after I did. She followed me home and we found him sitting at the table with his back to the door, going over the data from the Visitation as it scrolled across his laptop.

Davan didn't make a good first impression. His hair stuck up in a scruffy nest and his eyes were bleary from lack of sleep. He kept blinking and nodding as he read numbers aloud, muttering them under his breath.

"Dav," I said. "We have a visitor. The human kind; small 'v'."

"Power's out." Davan's head snapped up, just for a moment, before going back to the numbers. "Beer's in the sink with what's left of the ice. You'll want to drink it before it gets warm."

Chilli looked around our kitchen. Research HQ was a small shack at the back of Surfers Paradise, just far enough from the main drag to avoid the worst of the Visitation damage. Our kitchen was full of hi-tech junk: cast-off computer parts, Geiger counters and radio sensors, a couple of ancient seismographs Davan scavenged from somewhere and never got around to fixing up. There was a lot of ex-military stuff among the gutted PCs. Davan had a habit of adapting the equipment himself, forging a brave new form of technology to go alongside his research. I didn't understand it, just pressed the buttons he told me to press. Chilli gave it all a long, confused look, then shook her head. "I still need a drink," she said. "I'll ask about all this later."

We took the beer into the back yard and sat on the steps, the morning sun hidden by the low-set flats that surrounded us. This was the dive end of Surfers Paradise; all the buildings were decades old and none of them had the height of the modern high-rises. They were flats built in the era of soft pastels and poorly conceived signage, before beige became the default colour of everything on the Surfers strip and calling your holiday flats the Shangri-La Apartments became an exercise in irony.

"So, I'm Chilli. Hippy parents; don't ask." She offered me a hand and I shook it.

"Toby. The brain inside is Davan. You'll have to forgive him; he gets kind of intense for a day or so after a Visitation."

"I'll bet." Chilli drank her beer fast, wiping the residue from her mouth with the back of her hand. I handed her another and it went just as quickly. "Shit,' she said. "I mean, seriously, I always assumed you people were crazy."

Her eyes were kind of glassy by then. Shock was setting in.

"Yeah, I know." I shrugged and twisted the top off a third stubbie. "You're going to get that a lot now. Don't let it bother you. For all we know, we are crazy. We could be part of a global phenomenon that sees the same mass hallucinations."

Chilli thought about that. "I saw the footprints," she said. "There were big, fucking clawed footprints that sank a metre into the sand."

"Well, sure," I said. "There's stuff like that. But you'd be surprised what Normals write off as storm damage or pranks."

6.

Chilli didn't actually see a Visitor up close until Visitation G-31. She'd been hanging around the house for months, drinking beer and asking questions, doing her best to help out. Davan finally made the call to add her to the research team. I should have objected then, right when it started. Chilli had the look some Attuned get, that hungry need to see them up close. I didn't trust it in most people, but Chilli seemed cool-headed. Strong. I liked her, and I liked having her around, so I kept my mouth shut and let things slide.

Visitation G-31 was an airborne event, cruising over the Gold Coast before turning north and heading for Brisbane. No Attuned person in the city could miss it, but it was outside the range of Davan's equipment pretty fast. That meant we had to chase it if we wanted the data, so we piled into Davan's ancient Commodore with armfuls of cameras and black boxes. I let Chilli have the front seat; it gave Dav a chance to do his scholar thing. He loved lecturing to a captive audience, and he drove better when he wasn't trying to focus on something he couldn't see.

"Japan's been getting Visitations for decades," Davan said, getting into the groove of his lecture. We were cruising along the highway, dodging the cars that had slowed down for the storm. "Since the sixties, easily, but the Attuned numbers were low back then. Most of central Tokyo will see a Visitation now; the un-Attuned are in the minority. That's why they're so far ahead as far as countermeasures go. For them it's a matter of public safety rather than inconvenience. They have instances of wide-spread fatalities from time to time."

Chilli was nodding a lot, trying to stay interested. She kept looking out the window and scanning the sky. Reports had said the Visitor was some combination of pterodactyl and vulture, about forty feet long and violet. Rain splattered against the windscreen of the car, the windows misting as our combined body temperature raised the humidity.

"California is nearly as bad," Davan said. He kept his eyes locked on the road, trusting me to tell him when it was time to change direction. "It's the leading site of airborne Visitations across the board, even doing better than Dubai. Current theories suggest that the lingering concerns over earthquakes there make ground-based Visitations obsolete in the public consciousness. Miami—the American one, not the suburb—tends to have the big tyrannosaur types coming out of the ocean. Hawaii is much the same."

Something high above the car let loose with a sonic scream, high-pitched and shrill enough to make my skin crawl. Chilli looked up, her eyes a little wild around the edges. I tapped her arm and smiled. "Don't let him start about Hawaii," I said. "He ends up there twice a year for the conferences between Visitation academics. It's supposed to be a hot-spot of activity, but for some reason he never needs to take an Attuned assistant along on his trips."

Chilli flashed me a wan smile of thanks. Davan completely missed the irony in my voice. "Controlled experiences," he said. "They still have some of the smallest Visitations in the west, after Australia and the South Island of New Zealand."

"Tell her about the paper," I said. "The one by that woman in Milwaukee."

Davan started to speak, but the scream cut through the air again, louder and closer than the first. Chilli winced and raised her fingers to her ears. My own hearing buzzed in the aftermath; I could see Davan's head bobbing as he talked, but the words were a meaningless slur of noise.

"Pull over." I was shouting louder than I needed to and I could barely hear myself. Davan jerked the wheel hard and slid the car across the bitumen.

"We gotta go on foot," he said, passing out cameras. "Get whatever footage you can, and stay out of sight. It's supposed to be retreating, but don't take that as a given."

Chilli looked at the camera in her hand and frowned. "You're not serious, right?"

Davan was already out of the car, scanning the sky, trying to pinpoint the Visitor's location among the cracks of thunder and lightening flashes, hoping like hell he'd magically Attune. Chilli and I weren't as quick; the Visitor sounded closer than I was comfortable with, and Chilli was already starting to shake as she slid her hand around the camera's grip.

"Piece of cake," I said. "Find the critter, point the camera, run if it looks like it's coming towards you."

I climbed out of the car. I could see the Visitor immediately, about three hundred feet away, spiked tail flailing as it beat the air with leather wings. It had a horn sticking out of its head, something long and crystalline that glimmered in the dim light filtering through the clouds. It was heading east, back out to sea, its lavender skin stark against the dark clouds of the storm. I pointed the camera and hit record. Chilli got out of the car behind me.

"Holy shit," she said, her voice whipping past on the storm winds. "It's beautiful. And it's real." She pointed her camera, cackling, barely able to stand against the wind. Davan ran around, setting up his equipment. Cars sped past us on the highway, flashes of colour against the storm. "It's really real. I can see it."

"Is it still there?" Davan said. "Have we got it?"

Chilli and I didn't answer. We just stood there, cameras pointing, until the Visitor disappeared into the horizon.

7.

Davan has a video of the first Visitation. He isn't supposed to have it, but he'd tracked it down on the Internet. A contraband file the researchers swapped around in the name of science. We watched it one night, the three of us, drunk and bored, sitting around the television as it ran through the first Visitor's rampage across downtown Tokyo.

It was weird to watch, full of unfamiliar details. There hadn't been a Visitation in twenty years that wasn't accompanied by a storm, but in the Tokyo footage it's barely spitting. The Visitor itself is miniscule compared to their current Kaiju; barely big enough to pick up a car in its jaws. Chilli and I kept arguing about what it really looked like. We could agree that it was a giant lizard, covered in orange-red boils and translucent crystal spines, but the finer details were missing. Davan told us that Visitations were raw back then; that's why so many potentially Attuned dismissed them as figments or bad dreams.

The footage of Visitor Zero was taken on a video camera, an eighties betamax hunk-of-junk that kept flickering when it zoomed in for a close-up. Davan told us it'd been shot by an American tourist, some guy who happened to be Attuned and standing on the right overhead walkway, perfectly positioned to watch the carnage. Most of the crowd don't even see the Visitor, not even when it's bearing down on them. There were only a handful of Attuned back then, probably no more than six or seven hundred in Tokyo; a drop in the bucket when you think about the population of the city. On the footage, the few Attuned who are there keep trying to run, pushing their way through the rush hour crush. Every couple of seconds one of them keels over. Chilli and I could see them being roasted alive, caught in the radioactive blast of the Visitor's breath. Davan said they look like heart attacks to him, clutching their chests and falling to the ground.

The footage doesn't last very long. It's three and a half minutes before the Visitor turns in the camera's direction. You can hear the guy behind the camera screaming when he realises what's happening. The Visitor moves forward, jaws opening, and the yellow breath blasts out and all that's left of the footage is static.

"Shit," Chilli said. "That was intense."

She'd been seeing the Visitors for months by then, and she insisted on crashing on our couch most nights. She said it was because Davan had fortified the place, made it less likely to be damaged during a Visitor rampage, but I think she just wanted to stay close to the action.

Davan turned and looked at her for a few seconds, the ejected tape in his hands. "Hey," he said. "You want to come on a research trip? I'll be heading to Uluru next week. I need someone who's Attuned to come along."

"What about Toby?" Chilli said.

Davan looked at me and I shrugged.

"He's fishing for confirmation about his pet theory," I said. "I've already proven that I'm the wrong kind of bait." I figured it was safe enough to let her go. Davan had taken others out there, newly minted Attuned, and they hadn't heard a thing. Chilli shouldn't have been any different.

8.

Davan has videos of Chilli too. Old research interviews he taped on his shitty camcorder and transferred onto the computer. I hear him listening to them sometimes, her voice bleeding through the walls. Sometimes I'll go out and join him, watch Chilli's face on the screen. Old footage, before she cut her hair and replaced the lip-ring with something that wouldn't get caught in the field. Davan asks her what it's like, being attuned, and this digital ghost of her shrugs and looks to the right, smiling while she searched for an answer. "It's like waking up," she says, jabbing a finger at the screen. "It's like you realise all the things you knew in school, all the stuff they told you couldn't possibly be true; all the monsters under your bed and the imaginary friends and the magic pair of shoes you wore because they were lucky. It's like, suddenly, they're all real and you have to start believing in things all over again."

9.

They went to the Outback for a week. Chilli spent the day sitting on the couch after they got home. She'd stopped drinking by then. She just sat and smoked, letting her tea go cold and staring at the blue sky through the window. Davan didn't notice; he was too busy bubbling with excitement.

"She heard it," he said, shaking me as he bounced on the balls of his feet. "God-fucking-damn, Toby. She could hear it."

Then he showed me the footage. Eight hours of tape with Chilli describing the sounds. All the computer data he'd gathered by attaching electrodes to her skull. Davan took me through it, pulling things up on the laptop screen, jabbing a finger at things that were vitally important. "It's there," he said. "It's fucking there."

He disappeared into his lab. Chilli just sat, her eyes pale and empty. "You heard it," I said, and Chilli flinched. Her mug tipped over, dribbling the cold remnants of her tea down the side of her leg. I picked up the mug and steadied it on the threadbare arm of our couch. Chilli didn't budge. "Fuck, Chilli. This isn't good."

"It was…" she shook her head. "It wasn't horrible, but it was. You know?"

I tapped the cup with a fingernail. "I know."

"Why didn't you tell Davan?" she said. "All those times he's taken you out there, you've heard it, haven't you? Why didn't you let him know?"

I went into the kitchen and got some paper towels. I handed them over so she could sponge the tea out of her jeans.

"I had this friend once," I said. "Kenny. Back when I was eleven. His dad was a big guy. Ex-army, drank to excess, bit of a bastard, but likeable. Charismatic enough to disguise the fact that he was broken down, a little wrong in the head. I didn't get that at the time, not exactly, but I always knew something was up. It was in the air when you went round to Kenny's house."

Chilli dabbed at her jeans, pulling paper free of the roll. She nodded, eyeing me warily. I picked up the paper towels and balanced the roll between my index fingers, letting it spin when she pulled off another couple of sheets.

"Kenny's dad used to hit him. No reason for it, mostly, just an excuse to get his aggression out. I never saw him do it, but I saw the aftermath. We'd play quiet when we were at Kenny's house. We did our best not to wake his dad up, or do something that drew his attention.

"I've been to Tokyo," I said. "Way back, before Davan and I hooked up. It's got the same feeling as Kenny's house; they play quiet, waiting for the explosion, preparing for the inevitable."

Chilli dabbed and I sat there, watching the flickering static on the television. Davan was in his lab, replaying footage from the desert. It sounded low, deep and angry. A dozen snarling voices full of static and awkward harmonies.

"Aren't you curious?" Chilli said. "Isn't that the job? I mean, what's down there, it's like nothing I've heard before. And Davan—"

"Davan pokes things," I said. "He's a scientist, that's what he does; he wants to get something riled up so he can see how it works. I just want to play quietly, keep out of the way.

If the monster's content to sleep under the desert, then I'm not going to try and wake him."

She thought about that. "Safety isn't everything; Toby."

I should have heard it, then, the eagerness in her voice. I didn't. "Most of the time, it's enough."

"Whatever." Chilli threw the wadded paper towels on our coffee table. "I mean, you don't really think we can wake up whatever's living down there, do you?"

"I don't know." I pursed my lips, thinking it over. "No-one else has ever heard it. No-one else except you. I figured it was a question we never had to answer."

10.

I woke up at three AM when I heard something roaring. It was angry, but the rage was muted by distance. A Visitor call that didn't roll in off the ocean, the first time I'd heard one without the sound of rain on the roof.

Chilli was sitting on the couch when I emerged from the bedroom. She was watching the news reports about the storm brewing in the Outback. The Visitor's song got louder, a dozen voices joining in. Davan was still in his room, muttering in his sleep.

The next morning there was a news conference, and the government collected Davan so he could participate. Turned out every Attuned had heard it, thousands of people around Australia, with new cases hearing the Visitor's song every couple of minutes. "It sounds so sad," Chilli said.

'That's not a good thing. It used to sound alone."

We had dozens of Visitations over the next couple of weeks, Kaiju rampaging over the coastline as they pushed towards the red centre. Suddenly everyone was interested in the thing beneath the sand, wanted to know more about the song it was using to call its children home. Chilli and I didn't see Dana for days. The government had him sequestered somewhere, part of an ongoing task force. We'd get mysterious phone-calls when he needed something done.

"This is big," Chilli said. "You can feel it in the air."

She was right. Two days later Davan came home and warned us Visitation G-51 was coming.

11.

On the morning before 51 hit Surfers Paradise, Davan had us tying receivers to palm trees, making sure the microphones were clustered in the crook of the swaying fronds. None of the trees were solid enough to survive a run-in with a Visitor like G-51, but they were plants adapted to the high winds of a tropical storm. They had a better chance of standing up to the storm rolling in than anything man-made.

Chilli and I went and stood on the beach after we were done. We held hands and leaned into the winds, soaked despite the heavy raincoats and cold-weather jumpers. The emergency crews wanted us gone in a few minutes; we were only allowed there because Davan had insisted that we had to install his equipment. Chilli had cut her hair by then, shaving it down to pale tufts. She did it to keep hair from drooping into her eyes when it was wet.

The Visitor was just a shape out on the horizon; a dark shadow visible against the heart of the storm. It was hundreds of kilometres away, but you could still make out the shape: saurian, bipedal, blasting the air with quick flashes of lightning. We'd been listening to the radio while we were tying the mics down. There'd been record ocean swells in New Zealand and Cairns, towering sheets of water that were just shy of hitting tsunami levels. Most of the Pacific was bracing for the cyclone.

It was hundreds of kilometres away, but the Visitor still

seemed as big as my hand. I tried to guesstimate how big it would be when it arrived, but my brain kept refusing to hold the thought steady. Chilli swore loud enough to be heard over the storm. I looked at her and she leaned in, lips to my ears. "God," she said. "We're totally fucked when that thing gets here."

Her eyes were shining, aluminium bright. I smiled and gave her hand a firm squeeze. We were supposed to be far away by the time the Visitor hit the shore; out with the evacuees behind the mountains. Davan had organised everything as part of his research, and the authorities capitulated because they wanted his data.

Surfers Paradise was bunkered down for chaos. The beach was separated from the city by a thick wall of sandbags, three metres high and stretching off into the rain haze. The shops were closed and boarded against the weather. The high-rises were equipped with high-frequency beacons, designed to keep the Visitor from getting too close. All of it was rushed, techniques adapted from the Japanese. It would do fuck-all against the carnage an ordinary Visitor would wreak upon the landscape; it would do even less against the monster coming towards us. Still, they were trying. They figured they had to try.

Chilli checked the readings as they fed into her palm-pilot. "Five hundred clicks," she said. "About four hours away at his current speed."

"Assuming Davan's right about the water slowing its pace," I said.

"Yeah," Chilli said. "Assuming."

She took her hand out of mine and wiped the screen clear of water. I used my free hand to shield my eyes from the storm.

"Wind's picking up," I said. "We should start heading

off. There's supposed to be gusts of two-thirty kays an hour by the time it gets here."

Chilli nodded and put two fingers together at her lips. We retreated behind the sandbags and took cover from the increasing wind. I studied the sky, watching the storm-clouds boil.

"Has Davan checked in?" I said.

Chilli leaned against the wall, cupping her hands around a cigarette. It took six attempts to light it before the rain-blotched paper caught. The cigarette sagged in the middle, but she puffed hard against the damp tobacco. The ember bloomed for a moment and she exhaled a weak puff of smoke that swept off with the gusts.

"Davan?" I yelled again, and this time Chilli shook her head and started walking down the mall. It took me a couple of quick steps to catch up with her, my gumboots slapping on the brick-tile footpath. The high-pitched squall of the beacons left a weight against my eardrum, a buzz I couldn't quite hear.

The main drag was deserted, a thoroughfare dominated by palm fronds and stray garbage being swept along by the wind. I'd never seen the mall empty before, not even at four AM. Not even when the smaller Visitors came through, and the weather was so foul that no sane person, Attuned or not, went out amongst it. The entire place seemed peaceful; a twenty-four-seven suburb that was finally allowed to sleep.

"Listen," Chilli said, leaning close again. "Toby…when the time comes, you know, to get out of here…" She stopped, looked at the sodden cigarette wilting between her fingers. It was soaked through, the ember struggling against the rain. Chilli glared at it, shrugged and flicked the butt into a puddle.

"When the time comes?" I said.

Chilli looked up, surprised. It was like she'd suddenly forgotten she was speaking.

"Never mind," she said. Her eyes flicked backwards, towards the beach and the shadow on the horizon. "Sure is going to be a big fucker," she said. "I wonder what he'll look like, when we see him up close."

Her eyes were shining, ember-bright. The storm raged around us, pushing us away from the shore. I started heading towards the pick-up point.

When I turned around a few steps later, Chilli was gone.

12.

When the helicopter came to evacuate us, I was on it and Chilli wasn't. I'd like to think that wasn't Davan's fault, that it was all her choice to stay behind. That's possible, I think, but I don't have it in me to ask Davan for confirmation. He isn't exactly the type to volunteer an answer anyway, especially not now that they've given him a suit and a media advisor and a fancy government task force assigned to the Visitor problem.

The official reports list Chilli as presumed dead, but at this point finding a body is basically a formality. Davan struggles with it, blaming himself. He cries when he thinks I'm not looking, throws himself into his work when he's sure that I am. Sometimes he's gone for days at a time, off on research trips I'm no longer invited to participate in. Sometimes it's a media junket. Sometimes it's probably therapy. Davan's important now. He's close to eliminating the word 'Kaiju' from the Australian lexicon. They'll hold him together, one way or another and they let me cope in my own way, stoic and silent.

There's an investigation, of course; government men in bad suits who show up and ask questions, trying to work out why I let her go. They don't understand why someone would do it, giving themselves up to sit at ground zero, watching the Kaiju storm up over the beach. I give them copies of Davan's files, of all the footage where Chilli talks about seeing one up close. The investigators are always Normals; they never get it, but they nod and take notes and leave with their suspicions. There are days when I can convince myself it isn't Davan's fault at all. That Chilli chose to stay for other reasons, to finally see one of the visitors up close and personal.

At night I try to picture her in those final moments, waiting for the G-51 to hit. What it was like standing in the whipping wind, watching the concrete ripple like water as that first footstep rumbled through the city. Maybe she didn't live that long; the storms were bad before it hit shore; they got worse in the hours that followed the evacuation. I'd like to think she made it, though. That she actually got to stand there and look up at the towering lizard's presence, that she got to feel her heart hammer in her chest as it let loose that first toxic roar.

I picture her reaching out, fingers blistering as they get close to the beast's clawed foot, searing as they make contact for a few precious seconds before the winds and the storm whip her away and transform her into a name that appears on a government incident report. I picture her smiling in those last moment. I can't picture her doing anything else.

We know there are others coming now, other Kaiju working their way towards the desert and the small family of Visitors that roam the red sands. Whatever lives under the desert is calling them now, one by one, trying to bring them home. Davan's seen the reports; he goes quiet when I ask about them. "So many," he says. "So fucking many."

At night I sleep on the floor to avoid the worst of the tremors, the miniature earthquakes that roll through in the evening when the Visitors are most active. I listen to the song calling out from the desert, brutal and sweet as a lullaby, merging with the chorus of a dozen other Visitors that are calling, calling out, trying to draw their brothers home.

I may yet envy Chilli in those finals moments, the grandeur of her death. Until then I hope it was worth it, and I try to keep Davan calm on the days he's home, and I play quiet, oh so quiet, while I wait to see what's coming.

Dying Young

I smelled him coming long before he arrived, the musty odor of sulfur and dust cutting through the sweat-stink in Cassidy's Saloon. Smelling things is part of it, that thing I inherited from my Da, but it weren't just me who noticed it by the time he got close. The dragon stank bad enough that everyone breathed him in; the entire room hushin' up, listening to the tick-tick of claws on hardwood, lookin' at the door as he shouldered his way through.

He was a tall critter, but stooped over to fit his tail, and he'd been banged up good and proper by something a little more ruthless than the road. The wreckage that'd once been wings were folded over his shoulders, draped like a tattered coat. There weren't nothing but a jagged nub of bone where his horns had been, and that weren't good: Da once told me a dragon without horns got ornery, and they were usually trouble for more than just the feller what cut 'em off.

The dragon stared us down; no one said nothin' for a long stretch, but you can't stare at a thing like him forever. Someone up the back of the bar coughed, probably Sam Coody or one of his cloned deputies, and that was all it took for everyone to stop gawking and talk amongst themselves. The dragon sneered at us, showing off a ridge of serrated teeth, and walked over to the bar. We pretended we were okay with it, the dragon being there in the saloon, like it weren't no big deal, but our eyes drifted back. We watched him prop an elbow, easy as anything, and we waited for somethin' to happen.

The doc leaned over and nudged me with that big bone hook he calls a hand. "Trouble?"

I flinched 'fore I nodded, shying away from that hook. I didn't even need a vision to figure this one out; there was a gun belt hanging on the dragon's waist, visible every time he took a step, and Da never trusted strangers with guns. They were trouble, he said, and experience proved him right in the end. Doc Cameron knew that better than anyone.

The doc weren't satisfied with that, though. There were something pinching at the edge of his eyes, a little scent of fear underneath his oily perfume. "Look harder," he said. "Tell me what's coming," and he gave me a hard look, stared until I closed my eyes and peered forward, using Da's gift. I saw nothing but gray smoke, smelled nothing but fire. I could hear the sharp spit of an automatic through the haze.

"Something's burnin', I can promise you that," I said, "and I can hear a gun, Doc. Automatic. Someone's headin' for your slab, I think, before it's all over."

Doc Cameron half-lowered his eyelids and scratched the sharp edge of his cheekbone. Something flickered across his pupils, a cluster of lights spiraling towards the tear ducts as he scanned the dragon. Military tech, a hold over from the war, the doc's little gift to Dunsborough. The little box on his belt hummed, fixing the data from the doc's cortical patch onto a slice of silicon.

"Should we tell Coody, do you think?" I said, and the doc shook his head.

"The sheriff will want details," Doc said. "Damn fool won't run off a dragon based on a hunch, even one of yours."

The doc sniffed. Coody was Da's friend, last of the men Da trained before the doc took over. Doc closed his eyes and a light on the box flickered, the data loaded up and ready for study. "I'm going to go download this. Keep an eye on the lizard, Paul. The real eyes and the other. Maybe we'll get lucky."

The doc slipped out the back way, eager to get back to his lab. I sat and drank my sarsaparilla and watched the dragon like I was told. I kept one hand under the table, close to that sharp knife Da gave me when I turned fourteen. The dragon didn't do much beyond ordering whisky. I closed two eyes and opened the third wide, peering forward for all I was worth; it got me nothing but smoke and gunshots and the beginning of a headache that would last for days.

It weren't more than a half-hour after the doc scarpered before things got ugly.

I can see trouble coming 'fore most folks, even without the third eye. It was Da that taught me the trick of it, the ways of reading a room and seeing who'll make the first move. The dragon weren't lookin' for trouble when he first walked in, but he were waiting for some to roll on by and get itself started of its own accord. In the old days Da would've talked him around, but Da's long gone and Coody ain't quite got the knack of keepin' things peaceful. People in the bar worried, stayed quiet and whispered when they spoke.

It were Kenny Sloan who stepped up, stompin' across the floorboards to get in the dragon's face. Sloan's one of the doc's razorfreaks, a 'borg with a handful of scalpels and jacked reflexes, fast enough to slice the wings off a fly. He put his weight against the bar and looked over at the dragon, propping his arm on the counter so the light gleamed off the metal. Kenny Sloan was a bully, like most of the doc's boys. He flipped a quick grin back at his cronies, making sure they were watching. "Hey, lizard," Sloan said. "I thought your kind knew better than to drink at human bars."

The dragon turned then, mouth full of whisky, twin trails of smoke seeping out of its nose. The molten eyes squinted at Sloan, studying him. Sloan was a big guy, even before Doc jacked him up; no one missed him posturing. The noise died down and I saw Coody and his posse of badges straightening up in their corner, gettin' ready for real trouble. The dragon turned back to its whisky, ignoring us all. Sloan laid his fingers on the dragon's shoulder.

"Hey, lizard," Sloan said. He flicked the mechanical arm out, blades sliding free of the finger sheaths. "We already beat your kind once, yeah?"

Things happened fast after that, probably too fast to get the details without the third eye's hindsight. Sloan went to strike the dragon, Coody and his tin-star heroes got up on their feet, and the dragon moved faster than all of them. A quick twist away from Sloan's swipe, wings flaring out behind him, the dragon's stance was low with clawed hands splayed wide. Sloan got himself gutted before his finger-blades crunched into the top of the bar, and he stood there, bleeding slow from a stomach wound and struggling to get his hand free.

"You need a doctor," the dragon hissed. He swallowed the last mouthful of whisky, and Coody's men had him surrounded by the time he laid the glass down. The dragon eyed them carefully, all the sheriff's skinny mutant-clones with their clunky pre-war revolvers. Coody pulled Sloan's hand free of the hardwood; Kenny Sloan kept himself busy trying to hold in the mess of blood and gore that used to be his stomach. "Sorry for the mess," the dragon said, and he touched his blood-slicked claw to his forehead. His wings settled around him again, rearranging themselves to cover his gun belt and the sleek lines of his body. "I'll see myself out, yes?"

The clones looked at Coody and the old man nodded; no one said squeak as the dragon walked away. Sloan moaned a little, making gurgling sounds when he tried to speak, and as soon as the dragon was gone the sheriff looked around and pointed in my direction.

"Where's the doc?" Coody said. "Blood and thunder, son, go tell Cameron to hustle if he wants his pet 'borg to keep breathing."

I nodded and started moving, but Sloan was a goner. The doc didn't care about his 'borgs the way Coody looked after his clones, 'specially not when they were as dumb as Kenny and there was prey on the horizon. I went 'cross the square and buzzed the doc's doorbell, but there was no answer coming. I had nothing to do but wait, go back to Coody, or go trailin' after the dragon like I was supposed to. None of them appealed. Kenny Sloan was screaming inside the bar, dying slow and messy, so I went with the best option of the three; I ambled down the main street, following the soft buzz in my head that'd tell me where to find the dragon's camp.

The dragon was hiding out by Prickly Pear Hill, his bedroll stretched out in the middle of the twisted cacti that soaked up moisture from the stream curving 'round the base of the slope. He looked like he was traveling light; a small pack looked empty, like he'd been killing food on the march, but when I strolled in I got the familiar itch and saw dirt piled up where he'd buried supplies. I opened the third eye, peered on down, and got a sense of crates, canned food, and cordite.

I had myself a few good minutes before the dragon rolled

in, largely thanks to the fact that I weren't forced to backtrack in case the town sent out a posse. I sat on a rock and kicked the dust, listening hard, trying to hear him coming. It didn't work; I didn't hear him, see him, didn't even smell him this time around. I ain't easy to sneak up on, but he managed it. I just blinked my eyes and there he was, crouched low with claws out and hot spit dribbling down his chin.

"Boy," he said, nostrils flaring, and at that the smell of sulfur rose up around me. "You were at the bar, yes? Town sent you?"

I nodded, keeping my hands out in the open. I weren't armed with much, just my Da's knife, and it seemed to calm the dragon. He knelt down, sniffed me, then sighed a stream of smoke into the air. "Ah," he said. "You have gifts."

"A bit," I said. "Not much, not really."

He sniffed again, breathing deep. I recognized the trick from when Da used to do it, knew about the clues you could pick up with the right kind of training. The third eye does big things, its own special kind of magic, but Da always said there were other senses to fill in what the third eye can't see. The dragon smiled at me. "Trained, then? Your father?"

I shrugged the question away. "I work for the doc," I said. "He runs things; wanted you followed."

The dragon cocked its head, smiling. "Dangerous work, yes?"

I said nothing, just crouched there on my rock and waiting for what would come. I had enough of my Da in me to know I weren't going to die there, but that didn't mean I weren't going to pay hard for daring to follow him out there. I waited for the dragon to lash out, making use of his claws.

It ain't often I'm surprised, but he surprised me then. "I make tea, yes?"

"Oh." I blinked, and he watched me carefully. I forced myself to nod. "Yes. Please, yes."

I squirmed. The dragon turned his attention to the fire, hocked a sharp gob of spit into a pile of kindling to get things going. He unearthed an iron pot and loose tea from his pack, crouched down by the flames to set it boiling. There was something fascinating about the muscles moving under his scales, about the way sunlight gleamed on the dark ridges across his hands. He sat, dignified, and waited.

"You're after someone," I said. "I saw that much, back in the saloon. Can't see who, or why, but it's going to end messy."

The dragon kept its eyes on the tea. "Yes."

"I'm thinking it's the doc," I said. "He got plenty nervous when you showed up, hurried off to his lab right fast. That ain't like him, really. Doc Cameron likes his body parts, having new bits to play with."

That earned me a reaction, a snort of smoke and a twitch in the folded wings. "Yes."

"So what's going to happen, when you front up again?"

The dragon settled back on its haunches, stirring the pot. He lifted the pan and poured spiced tea into a pair of metal mugs, both of them bearing scorch marks on the rim. He handed one to me and I saw flecks of Sloan's blood drying on the dragon's claws. "You have the Sight," he said. "You tell me."

My forehead tingled, all prescience and instinct, but turned up nothing new. "I haven't seen yet; the future's nothing but smoke and gunfire." I took a long sip of the tea, felt the chili powder burning the back of my throat as it went down. The dragon watched me drink, red eyes narrowed to slits. I figured I knew what he was waiting for. "Ask," I said. "I ain't going lie."

"You have the sight, yet you work for your doctor?"

I guessed what he was asking and short-cut to the answer. "He did some bad stuff when he arrived," I said. "But good stuff, too. Helped people, gave 'em back stuff they'd lost. Relics of the war, sure, but they had arms and legs again. They could work, and we needed workers."

The dragon's laughter sent hot spit across the campfire. He put his cup down, tilting forward, and when he straightened up one of those ancient Lugers sat neat and easy in his hand. He pointed the narrow barrel in my direction, eyes narrowed down to stare at me. "You know, then," he said. "You've seen what your doctor has done?"

"Bits and pieces. Glimpses, really, but I got plenty of after what he's done since coming to town." I watched the cold fire in the dragon's eyes.

The dragon breathed deep. "He killed your father?"

I nodded again.

"And you work for him, still?"

"Sure enough."

"Why?"

"Needs to be done." I sipped my tea, staying calm; he wasn't going to shoot me, I could see that much. I don't have all my Da's gifts, not even half, but I was sure enough of that. "Not much good tellin' folk 'round these parts he's the devil; they need the doc too much to care and it ain't like anyone's goin' to be surprised by revelations of shady dealin's. And my Da didn't hold with revenge, really; he cared about keepin' folks safe. He would-a done the same as me, most likely, if he ain't ended up dead. These are nasty times; it takes a nasty man or a brave man to keep a town safe."

"Your father was brave."

"And look where it got him." I tried to keep the anger out of my voice, to avoid the flashes of history that rolled in if I let myself dwell on feeling. Hindsight can be a curse, Da said, and he weren't half wrong about that. "We're out of brave men, now he's dead. All we've got left is the nasty folk and the followers. Way I see it, I can have the doc dead or everyone else can live."

The dragon's expression didn't change and the Luger didn't waver, but the tattered wings rippled as he adjusted his stance. The crooked line of its broken horn caught the firelight. "What you have seen," he said. "You cannot save him."

I shook my head. "I wasn't lying," I said. "Haze, smoke, and gunfire, that's all I got; one of you will die, but I don't know who." I paused, drinking the last of the tea. "I got a fair guess about what happens next, though, after he's dead. It ain't pretty, not by a long stretch. Out here with nothing but Coody to keep things safe, it'll go downhill fast."

The dragon nodded, holstering the Luger and picking up its tea. "You should go."

I lingered for a moment, wondering what to do with my cup. The dragon rose, staring down at me. "Go! Tell your doctor I am coming."

I went, slinking back towards town with the tin cup still in my hand.

Coody's clones were manning the walls, so there was no real chance to sneak into town without anyone noticing. Two of them came down to the front gate to greet me, clamped down on my shoulder with heavy hands and started guiding me down Main Street. Four others stood on the palisade, dull eyes scanning the horizon while another one swept the landscape with the town spotlights. All of them tall, slack-jawed, armed; they looked the part, despite their daft expressions, hands on the holsters and eyes following the point of light that raked the landscape. The two walking me in said nothing, just held my shoulder and marched. I coulda given them the slip—Coody's clones aren't as bright as him, and he ain't exactly sharp as knives to begin with—but a trip to the sheriff's office gave me a good excuse to stay clear of the doc's lab and delay my report by a few minutes.

The original Coody was sitting on the porch of his office, whispering orders into a radio and making a big show of checking the action on the shotgun across his lap. He didn't even look when his clones threw me against the step, just pumped his gun with a satisfied grin and cradled it 'cross his lap.

"Sent you to go fetch the doc, Paul," he said. His good eye squinted as he drew a pistol and checked its load, the other glowing big and red beneath the doc's metalwork. "Cost us bad, you not doin' what I told ya. Sloan was dead 'fore the doc could get to him, nothin' left but parts."

Da tried training Coody, just like he trained me, but the sheriff ain't got none of the natural talent Da had for prescience or reading people. It made lying to him dangerous; he had to grind the answer out of you if he wanted to be sure of something.

"Called the doc and got no answer," I said. "He left me orders, 'fore he left for his lab, and I followed 'em when he didn't come to the door. You sayin' I done the wrong thing? That I shoulda' leant on his doorbell instead of doin' what he asked?"

"That's exactly what I'm saying." Coody's eyes scanned the town in a long, slow arc. "Doc Cameron's the brains behind this town, but I'm the law, kid. I'm the one who has to keep people safe now . . . " He cut himself off before he mentioned Da, took a deep breath to clear the thought out of his head.

I shook my head. "You really believe that, Sam?"

"Yeah, I do." One hand patted the shotgun and he looked at me for the first time, the mechanical right eye clicking as it focused on me. That eye was Doc Cameron's idea, a replacement for one Coody had lost during the last war. I was willing to bet that Cameron could see what Coody saw, if the doc had half-a-mind to check in. "What did the doc have you doing?"

I shrugged, and Sam Coody cuffed me across the back of the head. I went down in a heap, spitting red dust. "You wanna try that again, Paul?"

"He had me trailing the dragon." I sat up. "Wanted to know if it was after him."

"And is it?"

I nodded. "Close enough to."

Coody sighed and rubbed his good eye with his right hand. "So, you peered into the future on this one? It going to end bad, Paul?"

He held out his hand, helping me onto my feet. "It's going to end, Coody," I said. "I haven't seen spit worth talking about, but there's gunfire ahead and plenty-a screamin'. Dragon's got the sight, I think, an' he figures someone's goin' to die, but damned if I can see who."

Coody squinted. The long mustache twitched as he chewed on his bottom lip. He didn't say nothing for a real long time.

"I gotta report to the doc," I told him. "He'll be expecting me, Sam."

"Go," the sheriff said, and he went back to his guns.

No one likes going into Doc Cameron's bunker, least of all a guy like me, someone with the sight. Places like the bunker are always screaming, the echoes of the past ringing out again and again. But there isn't a damn fool in town that ain't carrying the doc's handiwork somewhere, not even me and I'm a damn sight cleaner than most, and Doc Cameron liked to keep tabs on folks. There were places I could hide, if I set my mind to it, but I'd come out eventually and pay my dues for disobeying him. I set across the square, and putting an eyeball to the scanner by the door, let myself into the bunker to tell the doc all the things he didn't want to hear.

My gut and my prescience both said it was a bad call; a braver man would'a skived off and spent the next day or three in his bunk, waiting out the storm until the shootin' was over. I wasn't a brave man, so I stood there until the steel doors swung open and a pair of Doc's razorfreaks fell into step behind me and escorted me through the winding tunnels Doc's boys hollowed out back when they first arrived.

The doc was down in his workshop, working on Sloan's corpse. He had the bone hook in the corpse's stomach, pulling down and opening the skin like a zipper. The smell of it made me gag, but he didn't even look up. "He's here for me, isn't he? The dragon?"

I looked over my shoulder at the razorfreaks, big lunks who stood there, uncaring and mute. Doc looked up from the slick gore of Kenny Sloan's innards, glared at me with cold eyes until I gave in and nodded.

"Who shoots who, Paul? Tell me how much it'll cost me to win?"

I closed my eyes and looked, hoping to get lucky: mist; gunshots; the screams of the dying. "I wish I knew, Doc."

Doc Cameron nodded and buried his long nose back in Sloan's vitals, poking about with the claw and good hand alike. His white coat was blood-splattered as he pulled the tech outta the dead. The days of the war were a long time past and supplies weren't comin' in; as the doc was fond of reminding us, it was a waste-not, want-not world now. He spooled cabling onto the slab, a thin line of plastic and fibers that had been in-and-out of 'borgs since the early days of the war. "You talked to the dragon, at least?"

I nodded.

"What did he have to say?"

"Not much." I fidgeted best I could between Cameron's guards. "He's coming for you, knew I had the sight. He wanted me to look into the past, get a good look at what you did during the war."

"And you did?"

"No."

Doc Cameron smiled. "You disappoint me, Paul. I thought you were built of sterner stuff." He stood up, abandoning his work. Sloan's guts dripped off the bone hook. He shook his head, full of mock sorrow. "What would your father think? A brave man like that, ending up with a boy like you?"

"I don't care what my Da thought, Doc. My Da is long dead."

"Why don't I believe you, Paul?" The doc's grin was terse, lips folded tight against his teeth. He held his bone hook like an offering, the oily smear of blood covering the tip. "Touch it, boy. Let us find out what kind of man you are."

Da used to say there were people who didn't come out of the war quite right, and there were pretty good odds the doc was one of them. I forced myself to look him in the eye. "Don't matter what you done, Doc. Not during the war, not last week, not when you first met the dragon and did whatever ya done to him. If you're the one who goes down . . ."

"Yes, if I go down." He let the thought hang, thin lips twitching, but neither of us finished it. He nodded to the razorfreaks and they hustled me out. I didn't bother struggling as they clamped their steel hands on my arms and lifted me, carrying me out.

．　．　．

The other freaks buried Sloan right on sunrise, interring the small bag of meat parts the doc couldn't use into the red dirt just outside of town. Coody and his clones watched things from the wall, stiff-backed guardians with shotguns and rifles, not wanting spit to do with the doc's bullyboys. They were allies, sure, when the town needed defending, but it was uneasy at the best of times and tense at the worst.

Coody doubled the guard that night. Buried meat had a way of attracting scavengers and things went downhill real easy after that happened.

My gut said we were safe for a day or two at least, and there were no tingling on the third eye to say it were wrong, so I drifted past Coody's office and let him know we had some time up our sleeves.

"Best keep an eye out," Coody told me. "Just in case, like." His logic was bravado, mostly, for all the truth of it. You didn't have to have the sight to feel the tension; the whole damn town was on edge, waiting, and Doc Cameron had been locked up inside his vault for nineteen straight hours trying to figure a way to save his skin. Da told me plenty of stories about his time in the army. Said we fought a whole damn war against the dragons and it'd cost us big every time the shooting started; one o' them might not seem much of a threat, but it was going to hurt everyone when he drifted through town again.

I spent the day in my bunk, trying to open the third eye or dream up a vision. Going forward got me nothing new, and going back taught me nothin' that I hadn't already suspected: Doc Cameron was never a nice man, and the war gave him ample chances to prove it over and over. He was cruel, yes, but I knew that, and there were lots more that seemed understandable given the cruelty goin' on back then.

And it's not like any of his habits changed much between the war and now, he just had fewer folk to experiment on and more opportunity for vivisection.

Coody came to see me, late in the afternoon. I didn't bother getting out of my bunk as he shouldered his way through the front door. He hooked one of my stools with the toe of his boot and slung it by the bed, settling down with shotgun still resting on his right shoulder. "You been lookin'?"

I nodded.

"You see anythin' yet?"

I shook my head and Coody grimaced, adjusting his weight on the stool. I saw one of his clones waiting by the door, smooth face filled with a slack-jawed grin as it kept watch on Main Street. It was Coody's face, but younger and dumber. The man sitting next to me was weathered and creased, carrying the weight of too many years. My Da's friend, a good man, doing his best in tough times.

"I was in the war with your father," Coody said. "Saw a damn sight more than I wanted to. Tangled with the dragons a couple of times before things went completely south. Whole damn race was human once, before they took to mutation. Damn things only exist because of folks like Cameron messing about with genes. Guessin' you're young enough not to remember that?"

I shook my head.

"Tough critters to face down," he said. "Fast. Strong. They smell you comin' before you even know you're goin' to draw. Saw a camp after the bastards attacked it one night. Lots of folks dead in their bunks—never heard 'em coming, motion detectors picked up nothing. You understand what I'm saying, Paul?"

I shrugged. Coody paused and took a long breath. "You've looked back, ain't you?"

I nodded, watching the gleam of Coody's mechanical eye, the way it whirred when he focused on me. I tried not to think of the doc watching me through it, listening in on the conversation.

"And the doc, he probably deserves what's coming, one way or another?"

I hesitated, just for a moment, then I nodded again. Coody sagged. "Damn."

There was a breeze outside, cold and gentle. I could hear the soft squeak as the wind-pumps in the town square dredged water out of the basin underneath the town. Coody leaned back in his chair, heel of his thumb working along the steel ridge of his bad eye. I twisted in the bunk, trying to get away from the dull red gleam as he stared at me.

"I ain't carrying a gun," I said.

Coody nodded. "I never asked you to."

"My Da . . . "

"Your father was your father, not you," Coody said. "You ain't him, Paul. I know that. He'd know it too, if he were still around. Things change, right enough, and you change along with 'em or pay the price." Coody pushed back on the stool, scraping it along the floorboards. I watched the red light of his eye bob as he pushed himself upright, shotgun sliding down into his hands. "D'ya know when the bastard's coming, then?"

I shrugged into the darkness. The night-vision optics installed in the eye would let Coody see the gesture. "Tomorrow, maybe the day after. He's got the eye, and he's better than me, I think. Good, as good as Da were. Makes it hard to predict him."

Coody grunted and thumped across the hut, settling in at the doorway to take a long look down the street. "Folks are goin' to die, Paul. Nothin' you can do about that. But if this thing's goin' to win, I want to know. Something's gotta protect this town, if the doc takes a bullet to the gut, and I ain't bettin' on the lizard to hang around to do the job."

I said nothing. There weren't much to say to that.

"I'm thinking of letting him through," Coody sighed, shifting his weight. "If we're lucky he'll come in quiet. Try and gut the doc and get out before anyone knows he's here. It ain't a nice idea, since it means losing the doc and all, but it'll keep some folk alive I reckon."

I thought about the dragon's camp: the cases he buried in the dirt, the dwindling supplies, his anger burning like kindling under a blowtorch. I shook my head. "He won't come quiet," I said. "He ain't planning on leaving anything behind after this is over."

"Even then," Coody said. "God help me, even then, it might not be a bad idea." He stepped outside then, saying nothing else, and I watched him go with a bad feeling in my stomach.

I made myself scarce after Coody left, grabbed my blanket and my Da's knife and left my shack behind. Sam Coody might not be askin' me to carry a gun, but the doc wouldn't hesitate if he got scared enough. People get confident when you put the sight and a gun together, like there ain't nothing to worry about if you can see what's gonna happen. Da's fault, mostly, 'cause he proved folks right around these parts, leastwise until the doc showed up. He did it here and he did it in the war, skated through everyone on sight and bravery. If Coody pulled the clones from the wall, left the dragon to the razorfreaks and 'borgs to deal with, you could bet Doc Cameron would call in every favor he had to save his skin.

Getting around town without being seen is easy enough if you've got the practice, 'specially once you know that the cameras you gotta avoid are stuck inside o' folk's heads instead of grafted to the side of buildings. I made for the water-tower on top of the saloon, wormed my way deep into the shadows underneath and hid there amid the splinters and the dust. It had a good view of the main street and I had a headache building up, a heavy weight that built up in the center of my forehead.

I slept there, fitful and quiet, away from where Doc and Coody could find me. I dreamt of Da on that last day, back when the doc first pulled into town. I dreamt of the future, of the dragon arriving, and heard a new sound among the gunfire: a sharp, wet bang, like someone 'sploding one of the paddymelons that grow down by the river, and Coody's headless corpse fell out of the smoke and lay smoking at my feet.

I woke up with the dragon crouched over me, his snout close enough for me to smell the sulfur. Gun in hand, eyes scanning the street. I stifled a scream and the dragon smiled. "You are hiding, yes?"

I coughed, soft and spluttering, before I said yes. The dragon peered across the street, watching the doc's muscle gathered 'round the bunker. Razorfreaks, the lot of them. Twenty men, maybe; all of them 'borged. "A lot of claws in those arms," I said. "Suicide to dive down and attack 'em."

The dragon just shrugged. "Yes."

"I had a dream." I pushed myself up on my elbows, whisper turning into a growl. "I don't know who dies between you and the doc, but I know who it costs us while the fighting goes down. The sheriff's going to let you in, assume you'll go quiet and leave everyone else alone. He figures there'll still be a town standing after you're done; that he'll protect the rubble from the predators and rebuild with the survivors."

"He is wrong," the dragon said. "It will cost him, yes? Boom, yes?"

"Yes."

He smiled at me, showing off the ridge of serrated teeth. "And so, you will stop me?"

I shivered despite the heat. "I don't think I can."

"You think," the dragon said. He shook his head. "You *think*."

I could swear the wheezing noise it made after that was something like a laugh. "You've got the sight," I said. "You know how this will end."

"I know," the dragon said. "I've seen my death."

"Don't do it," I said. "Please."

The dragon shrugged and checked the safety on his pistols. He squinted at the sun a moment, as though checking the time. "Is done," he said. "All done. There is nothing to stop it now."

I sniffed then, smelling him: brimstone and cordite.

There weren't anything quiet about the way the dragon was going down.

The first thing to go was the southern palisade. The rumble of the explosion rolled down the main street shaking red dust off buildings and rattling the windows. I was climbing down when it happened, got rattled off the side of the saloon and fell awkward in the dusty alley behind it. Pain rolled down my right shoulder as the screaming started out on the main street, people running for cover as the razorfreaks charged. I could hear the fight starting through the haze of smoke and dust: staccato bursts of gunfire; the cries of the dying, the dragon returning fire from his vantage on the rooftop. The doc's boys were fast and strong, but they weren't trained as much more 'n muscle. It'd take 'em a couple-a minutes to realize the shooter was somewhere up and outside the billowing cloud of smoke.

I scrambled to my feet and went for the wall, stumbling as the second bomb went off somewhere down the street. Dragons were quiet, Coody said, and hard as hell to detect; there'd be bombs all across town to create the distraction he was looking for, enough to flood the streets in smoke and fire, to ruin the infrared eyes the doc gave his razorfreaks to let 'em see in the dark. Coody and his clones gave minimal assistance, filling the street with spotlights while they took cover from the gunfire. They didn't move to help the razorfreaks, just dug-in and waited, a dozen of them with rifles not even looking for a shot. Coody stood behind the steel barrels of water we carted in from the reservoir, shotgun on his shoulder as he scanned the streets. The steel plate over his right eye shone in the light; he didn't notice me coming, not 'til I slid into place beside him. I yelled the word bomb, trying to get louder than the din. Coody nodded, looking irritated, and pointed at the carnage.

"Bomb," I said, screaming it, and pointed at his eye-plate. This time it sunk in, and he turned a little pale. I closed my eyes as another dynamite charge went off, caught a glimpse of the future. Clearer now, full of shapes, the sounds getting louder and louder as prescience became past. Coody ordered his clones into the street, ordered another two onto the walls to start searching the rooftops for the dragon and take him down with a rifle-shot.

I peered forward, snatching another glimpse. The gunfire and screaming in the smoke-haze started to die down. It was random now, scattered, the dragon picking the last of the razorfreaks off. My gut said we were out of bombs and out of mobs, so the killing would get real personal from here on in. I heard Coody calling orders, telling his clones to sweep the street, get survivors under cover and start putting out the fires.

I knew when I was going to die, if I didn't do anything stupid with my life. First trick Da taught me, when he figured out I had the sight. You look forward and you see your death, and you know that's how it'll end if you don't mess up destiny too bad in the meantime. The dragon knew it too, and so did my Da. It ain't writ in stone, but it's good enough. It takes some real stupidity to mess those visions up.

Da was supposed to die an old man, but he pushed things too hard. I was supposed to die an older man, and I hadn't pushed a damn thing, not since the doc came to town. I closed my eyes and looked, forcing my way through the smoke. Somewhere in the future the dragon was going to die and the doc would punish Coody for it. Or the doc was going to die and take Sam Coody with him. There weren't many ways it come out good for the sheriff, and there were a damn sight fewer where it came out good for the town.

I got out my Da's knife and stepped forward, walking into the smoke.

I found the doors to the doc's bunker open wide, the locks burned through with dragon-spit and smeared with oil and blood. I stood there a moment, breathing against a handkerchief to avoid choking on the dust. Coody stepped up beside me, shotgun in hand. "He in there?" he asked, and I nodded and tapped my nose. "Sulfur," I said, and went in, holding my knife out before me like it'd do a damn thing against anything we'd find running loose in the dark of the bunker. Coody followed on behind me, his mechanical eye clicking as it adapted to the darkness.

"You seen anything?" he asked me, "like, maybe, who's going to win?"

I shook my head, stepped over the body of a dying 'borg. "Get outta here, Sheriff. You don't want to be close to the doc today."

We heard a gunshot, deeper in, the sound of someone scrambling and running. Coody moved a little ahead of me, raised the shotgun. "It ain't exactly a choice, Paul. Dyin' comes with the badge."

He started moving in, gun at the ready, letting me follow behind. I tried to peek at the future, but there was nothing to see. Not anymore. Too many muddled pieces on the board, too many people trying to bluff and get a better result out of the hand fate dealt them. Occasionally we'd pass a body, see drips of blood on the concrete or smears of it on the wall. It's a twisty path, heading down to the doc's lab, and plenty of corridors leading off to the side. We found him hiding in one about halfway down, crouched in the darkness with a bone-saw in his fist. He was bleeding, the doc, but he moved okay when he saw us. "A grazing shot," he said, "lucky, at best."

"The dragon," Coody said. He pumped his shotgun for emphasis, chambering a live shell.

"Deeper in," Doc Cameron said, "there's a few boys towards the lab, trying to contain it." He paused a moment, stared at Coody. "They're doing your job, sheriff, unless I miss my guess. Perhaps you should go join them." There was steel in his voice as he said it, and his good hand at his belt hovering over the little box patched into his computer.

"The dragon's your mess," Coody said. "What if I say no?"

The doc's gaze slid over to me, then back up to Coody. "I gather you've been informed of that," he said. The laugh that followed was high-pitched, a trill of amusement.

Down the corridors, in the doc's lab, we heard someone screaming. "Probably best if you hurry," Doc said. He laughed again, winced, put his hook against the wall to steady himself. Blood loss, I figured. The scratch in his side weren't as minor as he made out. Prescience said the doc was already dead, just running out the final moments before the injury put him down. The only question now was whether the dragon and Coody went with him.

He wheezed for breath, leaning forward, and the hand over his computer box strayed a little too far. His eyes were stuck on Coody, waiting for the decision. I thought about Da for a moment, about dying old and safe, then I trusted my gut and Da's knife and went at the doc with a bloody yell and the knife twisting straight for stomach.

It cost me a hook across the face, stabbing the doc in the gut. He slashed me hard, but it didn't kill me; didn't even hurt when he followed up, jamming the hook in my stomach and ripping a shallow trench through the skin and the gizzards. The pain was bad, even looking back with hindsight, but I figure it was worth it. I got the knife in the doc two or three times in return, kept him busy while Coody lined up the shot and let the shotgun go boom 'til he ran out of ammo. I weren't conscious to see it happen, but the doc went down. Went down hard, a bloody mess, and Coody standing over him with the gun just-in-case, calling down the clones to stitch me up and get me walking.

I spent a week or two in bed, healing up from my injuries, and would have myself some nice scars to show off by the time I was healed. The dragon was gone by the time I came to, walked out of town by Coody with supplies and a warning. There weren't much left for him in town, with the doc laid out for burial, and there were plenty of folks out for his blood after the business with the explosions. He went quiet, which surprised me, and he was missing an eye to go with his broken horn.

We were due some hardness, everyone knew that, and there were a couple-a folks held grudges against Coody for doing in the doc. But we held off against the scavenger beasts and the retaliatory raids by the last of doc's 'borgs, found ways to make do when his tech ran down and people started limping 'round town on malfunctioning limbs. I started wearing my Da's gun, when Coody asked me for help. He was running short of clones, now. There were men in doc's labs trying to fix the machines, but they weren't none as smart as him and it would take a while to get things running, if they ever did.

Things are good, though, since the dragon came. Tougher, yes, but not so bad as they were. My Da used to tell me that people cope, that the war proved that more than anything. But they'll do more than cope, if you ask them too, if you show them there's another option. That they'll do the right thing, eventually, 'cause doing otherwise there ain't much to life. I'm not saying he were right, mind, but he saw a lot of what might happen. He was a smart man, Da, and he were better at lookin' forward than me.

But that was him, and he did his part. Now there's me and Coody and a bunch of broken parts, a town that needs savin' and a future stretchin' forward. And maybe I get to make it to the end I'm meant to have, and maybe I get sidetracked a little along the way. It doesn't seem so bad, not knowing, not like it used too.

And Da always used to tell me there were worse things than dying young.

ONE SATURDAY NIGHT, WITH ANGEL

I am not at my best in the mornings, so I've spent much of life getting acquainted with the kinds of utilitarian places one goes late at night. This means I've spent far more time hanging out around convenience stores, laundromats, and 24 hour service stations than is fiscally sensible, taking care of errands that couldn't be done in the limited amount of daylight hours available to me.

Part of this story is built around my affection for these late-night, liminal spaces. The other half comes from researching gargoyles, gothic architecture, and all the myriad ways public spaces are manipulated to make us think about our mortality and morality, then trying to figure out ways to apply that to the Brisbane landscape.

TO DREAM OF STARS: AN ASTRONOMER'S LAMENT

Every six months or so, regular as clockwork, I used to get an email from a high school student asking me to explain the meaning and imagery in this story. It confused me a lot, until I found out that an excerpt had been included in some HSC prep asking them to write a critical response.

I would frequently write back and point out that authors thoughts on a story rarely coincide with what English teachers are looking for, then pointed them towards some of the cultural theorists I was reading back when I first put the story together. Eventually the emails came often enough that I wrote a blog post with my standard response, attached a click-bait title, and let Google take care of things.

There is a lot of things underpinning the story, but what I don't mention in that post is my fascination for the era where faith and science went hand-in-hand. This wasn't meant to be a story about those two things, but it quickly became one as I started fleshing out the drafting.

THE LAST THING SAID BEFORE SILENCE

A friend invited me along to a screening of classic French films, which included Albert Lamorisse's *La Balloon Rouge*. It's one of those movies that has permeated the culture, the image of the boy and his red balloon repeated over and over, but there was something about the original and its seemingly sentient balloon that jarred an idea loose in my head.

Lamorisse's film is a comedy, of sorts, but the line between comedy and horror is so very short and largely a matter of perspective.

This was published in *Weird Tales* 357, during Ann VanderMeer's editorial tenure, both of which made me extraordinarily happy. I grew up as an RPG gamer, immersed in *Dungeons and Dragons* and *Call of C'thulhu*, which means *Weird Tales* has a special place in my heart and getting published there was a dream my twelve year old self wouldn't have dared to dream.

THE GIRL IN THE NEXT ROOM IS CRYING AGAIN

There are two places this story began. The first involves explaining ESP to someone not particularly immersed in speculative fiction and, for the first time in years, found myself spelling out the acronym instead of settling for short-hand. I'd gotten so used to thinking in terms of telepathy and mind-reading that I'd lost track of the sensory aspect, and I started thinking about the ways smells and tastes evoke memories we'd otherwise forgotten.

The other place was that period in the early 2000s when Urban Fantasy, as a genre, seemed to coalesce into a genre that blended fantasy and hardboiled detective fiction or noir. Everything I was reading drew heavily on the Raymond Chandler tradition, where the detective was still marked by a streak of honor and nobility, ignoring the long tradition of noir plots in which flawed characters attempt to do something right and achieve, at best, a Pyrrhic victory.

The result is not a particularly nice story, and it's filled with not particularly nice characters who are destined for a bad ending.

SAY ZUCCHINI, AND MEAN IT

Words are slippery fuckers. You can flip through the dictionary all you want, looking at those nice clean definitions, but in truth those don't mean much. Words, on their own, mean nothing without context - it's only the other words in a sentence that tell you whether bat means "winged marsupial" or "sporting implement."

It's only who you're saying it too – your partner, your lover, your sibling, your grandmother – that clearly identifies what you may mean when using the words "I love you."

Fiction and film has played with the subtle ambiguity for years, presenting who says I love you and how as a potential course of conflict.

I figured the logical conclusion to all this was making the words physically dangerous to say, and start figuring out how that would change our lexicon.

CLOCKWORK, PATCHWORK, & RAVENS

I wrote this story at Clarion South in 2007, where it benefited from the critique and advice of several instructors and a cohort of instructors. It was published in Apex Magazine two years later, then went on to pick up the Aueralis Award for Best Science Fiction Story that year.

I set out to write a cyberpunk story where the protagonist was invested with a kind of fairy-tale innocence, creating a contrast to the raw cynicism that lies in the roots of cyberpunk's neo-noir trappings. This tended to pull all the technology in a similarly archaic direction, resulting in high-tech clockwork and genetically engineered corvid gangs.

52 PICK-UP

This shares a world and a peripheral character with *The Girl In The Next Room Is Crying Again,* and a similar interest in unpleasant people dealing with their frustration, anger, and guilt. It's built around my memories of two nightmarish hours spent commuting between the Gold Coast and

Brisbane back in my early twenties, when every conversation going on around me seemed ranged from unpleasant to goddamn terrifying.

MEMORIES OF CHALICE

The city of Chalice has its origins in a stock image someone used for a writing prompt, years ago, and everything else in the story seemed to accrete around it as I pondered why someone would build a seemingly modern city in the heart of a crevasse.

The initial foundation took about a week to get down, but the bulk of the story took several years to flesh out and get right. The final piece didn't slot into place until just prior to publication, John Klima was doing his editorial pass prior to its appearance in *Electric Velocipede* and pointed out that there was something not quite right about the original opening line.

I immediately sat down and wrote the current opening, then realised how much easier the whole writing process would have been if I'd come up with that particular metaphor right at the beginning.

FROM TUESDAY TO TUESDAY

I once rented a house with a bathroom at its heart, the small room with its tub and shower existing as a small island separated from every other room by a hallway on all sides. It was one of the oddest bits of architectural design I've ever encountered, and I kept thinking about it long after I moved it.

This story vegan when I started imagining who inhabited that house long after I left, and what their lives would be like.

INSIDE AN EGG, INSIDE A DUCK

I wanted to do a science-fiction take on one of my favourite fairy tale tropes, although the results were much less science fiction than I'd hoped for.

VISITORS

There are stories that come together easily, everything slotting into place through the writing process.

This story is not one of those.

It started incubating in my head back in 2005, when the bulk of my writing was still focused on RPG games instead of fiction. I'd seen an open call for kaiju stories from the editors of the *Daikiju: Gaint Monster Tales* anthology, Rob Hood and Robin Penn, and was dimly aware that I'd like to try writing fiction.

I wrote a thousand words, maybe, then went back to writing the things that were paying the bills back then.

Fast forward to 2007, when I'd seen the writing on the wall for my RPG gigs and gave fiction another try. I went to Clarion South, a six-week writing workshop, and Rob Hood was one of the instructors. We talked giant monsters, and I remembered this idea kicking around, so I figured I should finish it now that I was giving fiction more time.

It still didn't work.

For three or four years after that, this was the story I'd pull out and tinker with whenever other stories weren't coming together. I'd do a scene here, add a detail there, gradually flesh it out until it started to look more and more story-like.

It eventually got published in a very different theme anthology, Tehani Wesseley's *After the Rain*, in the same year that Brisbane was devastated by city-wide flooding.

DYING YOUNG

I like writing longer stories and novelettes, but they're generally a bugbear to get published. The idea of bringing together dragons, cyborgs, psychics, and gunslingers had been kicking around my hard drive for a few years, but it took Jonathan Strahan's invitation to submit something to the fourth Eclipse anthology before I had the space to write the story I wanted to write with the idea.

Then, it came together faster than any other story I've written, buoyed by my sheer glee at getting to play with the various genre elements. Then I hit the title and just ran out of steam, which meant I tried various alternatives that didn't quite fit. In the end it went out with the second working title in place (the first was cyborg-dragon-psychic-western-wahoo story, which is not the kind of thing that looks great on tables of contents). It went on to become the most reprinted story I've written over the years, and remains one of my favorites.

Actually, speaking of favourites, I'm going to sneak one last story in here at the end as a bonus for those who read the notes until the bitter end.

This is one of the first pieces of fiction I had published - a flash story I wrote the first Christmas I lived alone and realised how quiet the world got around the holidays.

THE YEAR THE ZOMBIES CAME FOR CHRISTMAS

It was Katie that remembered the puppy, trapped in its cardboard box without any air-holes. The fact that we'd forgotten to punch any in came to her at 2 am, a surge of panic that sent her upright in our bed.

"It's cardboard," I said. "It's not like the damn thing will suffocate. We'll make sure Steve opens it early, before any of the other presents."

That calmed her down a little, though only just. She fretted, because fretting is the kind of thing Katie does, but the puppy was downstairs and Steve was a notoriously light sleeper. Another trip to adjust the presents, past the creaking floorboards in the hall, was likely to wake him. We didn't want that, not when we were holding onto his tenuous belief in Santa Claus by the skin of our teeth.

So we left it; a puppy in a box that was carefully wrapped in a blanket to muffle stray barks and covered with purple wrapping paper.

Neither of us had grown up with pets. The dog was foreign to our experience of the world, an idea embraced for its old-fashioned charm. I imagine that it whimpered in its final moments, before the fear and the darkness overtook it. Before the breath locked in tiny lungs and it lay down for what should have been a final rest. Sometimes, when I remember that last Christmas Eve, I feel a pang of sympathy for the puppy's lonely death.

Christmas Morning is an insular time, cut off from the rest of the world. We slept late, waking to Steve's CD full of Christmas carols rather than the six AM news. There were no newspapers to collect, no job luring us out of the house within the space of hours.

There was no reason to suspect anything was amiss when the puppy's box started twitching.

Several of these stories have appeared elsewhere, in some cases in a different form:

- "One Saturday Night, With Angel" © 2008 Peter M. Ball. First published in *Sprawl*, ed. Alisa Krasnostien (Twelfth Planet Press),
- "To Dream of Stars: An Astronomer's Lament" © 2009 Peter M. Ball. First published in *Apex Magazine*, September 2009
- "The Last Thing Said Before Silence" © 2011 Peter M. Ball. First published in *Weird Tales 357*, Spring 2011
- "The Girl In The Next Room Is Crying Again" © 2011 Peter M. Ball. First published in *Daily Science Fiction*, December 2011
- "Say Zucchini, and Mean It" © 20011 Peter M. Ball. First published in *Daily Science Fiction*, May 2011
- "Clockwork, Pathwork, and Ravens" © 2009

Peter M. Ball. First published in *Apex Magazine*, May 2009.

- "52 Pick-Up" © 2018 Peter M. Ball. Original to this collection.
- "Memories of Chalice" © 201 Peter M. Ball. First published in *Electric Velocipede #21/22*, February 2011
- "From Tuesday to Tuesday" © 2013 Peter M. Ball. First published in *Daily Science Fiction*, November 2013.
- "Inside an Egg, Inside a Duck" © 2018 Peter M. Ball. Original to this collection
- "Visitors" © 2011 Peter M. Ball. First published in *After the Rain*, ed. Tehani Wesselly (FableCroft Publications)
- "Dying Young" © 2011 Peter M. Ball. First published in *Eclipse 4*, ed. Jonathan Strahan (Night Shade Books)
- "The Year The Zombies Came for Christmas" © 2007 Peter M. Ball. Dirst published in *Antipodean SF #105*, Feb-Mar 2007.

I sat down to write my thank-you for the folks who helped with this collection, then realized that it's largely the same crew of people who helped put together my last collection. No writer truly works in isolation, and I owe a considerable debt to all the friends, editors, writers, co-workers, and housemates who offered support, feedback, and encouragement over the years.

I will note that a considerable number of these stories were written at or immediately after Clarion South 2007, and benefited from the critiques and camaraderie of the organizers, tutors, and my fellow attendees.

Particular thanks go out to the following people:

- The inimitable Angela Slatter, write club buddy and one of the smartest writers I know.
- Sarah Blue, who spotted a couple of goofs I'd missed while moving the manuscript around the coffee table
- Adam Windsor, who let me camp out in his spare room for significantly greater period than was

truly sensible during the period where some of these stories were written.

- The staff and student body of the Griffith University Creative Writing program, who gave me the opportunity to both learn about the short story and teach others about them as well (and really, teaching is just another kind of learning).
- The team of the Queensland Writers Centre.
- My parents, Terry and Margaret Ball, and my sister, Sally Ball, who have put up with this craziness for far longer anyone else
- And, as always, all the editors and slush readers who worked on the magazines and anthologies where many of these stories first appeared, and those who have reprinted these works in the years since they first appeared.

PETER M. BALL is an author, publisher, and RPG gamer whose love of speculative fiction emerged after exposure to *The Hobbit*, *Star Wars*, David Lynch's *Dune*, and far too many games of *Dungeons and Dragons* before the age of 7. He's spent the bulk of his life working as a creative writing tutor, with brief stints as a performance poet, gaming convention organiser, online content developer, non-profit arts manager, GenreCon convenor, and d20 RPG publisher.

He's the author of the Miriam Aster series and the Keith Murphy Urban Fantasy Thrillers, three short story collections, and more stories, articles, poems, and RPG material than he'd care to count. He's the brain-in-charge at Brain Jar Press, and resides in Brisbane, Australia, with his partner and a very affectionate cat.

Want to get in touch?
www.petermball.com

Or reach out to Peter on your favourite Social Media platforms:

facebook.com/PeterMBall

twitter.com/PeterMBall

instagram.com/PeterMBall

goodreads.com/PeterMBall

patreon.com/PeterMBall

ALSO BY PETER M. BALL

EXILE: A Keith Murphy Urban Fantasy Thriller

**Keith's been in exile for sixteen years.
Today, he's going home.**

When a botched hit leaves Keith Murphy on the run with a necromancer's soul trapped in a bullet, he makes a beeline for the one city where it's impossible to track him using magic. Problem is, the Gold Coast is ruled by a demon whose been nursing a grudge ever since Keith crossed him, and the old friends and allies he counted on helping are none-to-pleased to see Keith home.

A fast-paced Australian urban fantasy thriller full of magic, demons, betrayal, and deals with the devil. If you ever wanted a little John Constantine blended in with John Wick, you're going to love Keith Murphy.

Read on for a taste of *Exile*…

A fast-paced Australian urban fantasy thriller full of magic, demons, betrayal, and deals with the devil. If you ever wanted a little John Constantine blended in with John Wick, you're going to love Keith Murphy.

They found me in the Hard Rock. Thursday night, a little after ten. The bar drew a good crowd for a Thursday, all things considered. Lots of girls with inscrutable, backpacker accents clustered around the counter. Plenty more heading for the Beer Garden upstairs, attracted by the cover band's caterwaul. Blondes, legitimate and peroxide — a Gold Coast epidemic. Swathes of exposed skin, despite the cool nip in the air. Twenty-dollar cocktails named after natural disasters: Typhoons; Tsunamis; rum-soaked Hurricanes.

I'd racked up three straight hours sitting in the downstairs bar, drinking short blacks and reading my book. A guy flying solo at a cozy table for four, ignoring the crush of the late-night crowd, the heady mingling of sweat and perfume and the salt-water from the nearby beach. I blew off the irritated, dark-eyed waitress who kept offering to take my coffee cup in the hopes I'd fuck off and free up the four top. I wasn't waiting for anyone else. Just me and my beat-up copy of *Persuasion* on yet another stake-out, killing time until the local talent picked up on my presence.

I'd selected a table up the back, wedged between one of

Keith Moon's polyester shirts and Mark Occhilupo's surfboards. Earlier, when I'd been eating dinner, tourists stopped by to read the brass plaques and sniff at my empty seats. Personally, I didn't give a shit about the memorabilia. My position delivered clear sight-lines on the bar, the gift shop, and both sets of sliding doors.

The band working upstairs distracted me with their off-key singing and affection for the Gunners. Every time they launched into another cover, I'd lose my place and have to re-read the same page of *Persuasion* again. I'd stumbled over the same line about fine ladies and calm waters ever since their version of 'Knocking on Heaven's Door.' They were leading the bellicose crowd through the chorus of 'Paradise City' right as the demon walked in.

His arrival marked the end of my reading. I downed the dregs of my coffee and watched the big feller work. The purposeful stroll through the gift shop, all swagger and white teeth. The momentary pause as he scanned the room with a jungle cat's poise, making a note of every warm body crammed in among the memorabilia. I figured him for six-nine, give or take an inch. Athletic and well-built, dressed to fit in with the local crowd. Tight black jeans and bright red high-top sneakers, a walnut tan just brown enough to be real instead of spray-on.

The kind of guy I'd remember, even after sixteen years, and I couldn't recall anyone with his height and frame among Sabbath's mooks. New blood, then. Definitely a demon. I didn't need to pierce the veil to confirm it — he carried himself in that languid, unsettling way most creatures of the Gloom deploy when they forget to play human.

The short, dark-eyed waitress stopped by my table and removed the empty coffee cup. Asked me if I'd like another, and broke into a grin when I told her I'd finish up soon. I pulled a twenty out of my wallet, folded it, and slid it beneath the salt and pepper shakers. Dog-eared my current page and stuffed *Persuasion* into a jacket pocket so I wouldn't leave it behind. Things would start moving fast now a demon was on the prowl.

He crossed the bar at a leisurely pace, stopped to chat up women and deploy a toothy smile. The first three shot him down, which took effort on his part. Demons flirt easier than most people breathe, and this guy's jaw and build were easy on the eyes. In the fourth he found a receptive partner, the kind of chick young men dream of meeting at a joint like the Hard Rock: bleached-blond; white t-shirt; tanned and smooth and friendly, her cut-off jeans showing off the pink hibiscus tattooed on her right thigh. Her intentions were obvious in the raucous laugh she deployed, and her drunken lurch into the demon's side.

Then the Big Guy glanced my way, a surreptitious glance to confirm I'd clocked his presence. Could be a subtle warning to back off and let him feed in peace, or a predator recognizing a potential threat and disregarding it before hunting. And so we kicked off a round of my least-favorite game, trying to figure who was playing who.

The blonde made it easy for the Big Guy. Pressed against him, whispered into his ear. Midriff top giving him access to bare skin as he pulled her close. The veins closest to his fingertips turned dark as he siphoned a fragment of her life-force. He did it light and subtle, like a pickpocket filching your wallet. The drain left the girl woozy, bought the demon a chance to prop her against the bar and scan the crowd for another victim.

Slick work, and feeding in public is brazen for any demon. This guy played it cool, focused on the prey. My presence forgotten or disregarded, confident I wouldn't risk a move on Sabbath's turf and put a target on my back. Given the way possession enhanced human senses, he already knew

I wasn't local. My scent was fresh off the Greyhound, a sour-and-rumpled traveler who'd gone too long without sleep. My flannel shirt too warm for the Gold Coast summer, but ideal for covering the the tethers inked along my arm and the SIG tucked into my belt.

I tracked his movements, trying to figure out if he was overconfident, dumb, or extremely good. Realized too late he was the fourth option: a big, distracting billboard deployed to capture my attention. When the .38 kissed the hollow of my back, just below the ribs, a part of me was flattered I'd warranted that kind of caution from two alpha predators.

Of course, that part of me was dumb as rocks, but I guess nobody's perfect.

Wesna Holjack leaned over my right shoulder, her voice tickling my ear. "Well, shit, Keith Murphy. How the fuck are you?"

"Hey Wes," I said. "Been a while, yeah?"

"You think?" She slid into the empty seat beside me, draped her arm around my neck. The other hand jammed the pistol into my gut, made it clear trying to squirm or run would trigger a messy response.

"You should have left it longer," Wesna said. "Now I'm kinda pissed I have to kill you."

EXILE and the other books in the Keith Murphy sequence are available now. Order it direct from Brain Jar Press or find it in your favourite store today!

Thank You For Buying This Brain Jar Press Chapbook

To receive special offers, bonus content, and info on new releases and other great reads, sign up for our newsletters.

To get more from the author, Peter M. Ball, you can sign up for his newsletter at PeterMBall.com

To get the latest updates form the publisher, Brain Jar Press, you can sign up at BrainJarPress.com

www.ingramcontent.com/pod-product-compliance
Lightning Source LLC
Chambersburg PA
CBHW020807190726
48285CB00006B/2191